The Time Capsule Diary

By Rachel R. Reichl London

The Time Capsule Diary by Rachel R. Reichl London

Copyright © 2019. All rights reserved.

ALL RIGHTS RESERVED: No part of this book may be reproduced, stored, or transmitted, in any form, without the express and prior permission in writing of Pen It! Publications. This book may not be circulated in any form of binding or cover other than that in which it is currently published.

This book is licensed for your personal enjoyment only. All rights are reserved. Pen It! Publications does not grant you rights to resell or distribute this book without prior written consent of both Pen It! Publications and the copyright owner of this book. This book must not be copied, transferred, sold or distributed in any way.

Disclaimer: Neither Pen It! Publications, or our authors will be responsible for repercussions to anyone who utilizes the subject of this book for illegal, immoral or unethical use.

This is a work of fiction. The views expressed herein do not necessarily reflect that of the publisher.

This book or part thereof may not be reproduced in any form, stored in a retrieval system, or transmitted in any form by any means-electronic, mechanical, photocopy, recording or otherwise-without prior written consent of the publisher, except as provided by United States of America copyright law.

Published by Pen It! Publications, LLC
812-371-4128 www.penitpublications.com

ISBN: 978-1-952011-83-2
Edited by Peggy Holt
Cover by Donna Cook

Dedication

I would like to dedicate this novel to my amazing family, especially my mother and late father for pushing me to always succeed in everything I do or aspire to do. This book is also dedicated to my amazing close friends Alisa, Maddie, Stephanie, Sharmey, Lynn, Amalia and all my anxiety group friends for always pushing me and believing in me. I also want to dedicate this novel to Lori, Sandy, Peggy, Donna, Donna, Sue, Lisa, Stephanie, Cheryl, Lauren, Lisa, and Rebecca, who are my favorite receptionists, hairstylists and nail techs who always support me and make me feel welcome when I go visit them at the hair salon. Last but not least I want to dedicate this book to my library friends. You guys are the best and I love working with you every week. Thank you all for all your support it has meant and still does mean the world to me.

Before School and the School Years

Dear Diary,

    Hi, my name is Gracie Elizabeth Paris Amethyst and this is my story. I thought I would begin this diary time capsule by introducing myself to all of you lovely readers and give you some context as to why I am doing this. I am doing this so that generations of the family can get a bit of family history, and so I can share with you what it was growing up in a not always warm and welcoming world as a woman with Autism.

    You are probably wondering where all these stories and memories that are written in this diary came from. They came from my old diaries which I found while cleaning out my attic, and after perusing through them I decided to use the events that I wrote about through my childhood, and adulthood to help me tell the story. I also thought I should give a fair warning this diary has time jumps and each diary entry talks about a different time in my life. I did this so that I could put the entries into chronological order so that it would be easier to follow and it makes it more interesting and fun.

    To begin this story I should probably tell you what Asperger's Syndrome is, Asperger's Syndrome is a high functioning form of Autism. Being a girl with autism in my town meant many people made assumptions about me without really getting to know me. People would often say that I was rude or lacked dripline and manners, which wasn't true. Since I did not want to feel, weird or different I created an imaginary world where I felt safe and understood. No one judged me or made fun of me there and I could be myself without embarrassing my family. Being there was awesome and magical because I was always going on great adventures and I was always the hero. I loved playing there and always managed to be braver there then I was in real life. In real life I was shy and often kept to myself because it was safer that way. It was easier to be brave in my imaginary world because, the worst that would happen was I had to save the world from a dragon or an evil wizard or something.

When I was not in my imaginary world, the place that I loved to explore this world the most was my house. I lived at 97 Spring Rd with my loving parents and my seemingly perfect older brother Jason. Our neighborhood was quiet and peaceful for the most part except for the occasional car or motorcycle driving down the street. It was the perfect suburban neighborhood, with lots of oak and maple trees and an apple orchard down the street. Some of the neighbors were stuck up but others were pleasant and benevolent. However we all pretty much just kept to ourselves and only really talked to each other when it couldn't be avoided. The houses on the street varied from nice classical colonials to ranch style homes.

I especially loved our house, which was gray with blue shudders. I also loved the beautiful oak trees, maple trees and the sweet-smelling pine trees. The oak and maple trees were perfect for climbing as long as I had some help getting back down. The pine trees smelled like Christmas and it was fun walking through them in the woods behind my house. Being at home was my safe place. What I mean is when I was home; I could do whatever I wanted as long as I did not hurt myself or anyone else.

Sometimes when I would leave the safety of my house, both strangers and people who knew me treated me like an outcast or a town freak. They would stare and sometimes make snide remarks towards me and my family because they did not understand why I was acting a certain way. I did not mean to embarrass my family but sometimes it happened anyway. I always felt guilty about it but my parents and brother always understood.

One time while my family and I were at a local Italian restaurant, I was acting out a little bit because I was bored and hungry and growing more and more impatient. My parents were trying to calm me down so that people would stop staring. As they were staring at us, an ignorant woman asked my parents if they did anything to make me act the way I was acting. After seeing the embarrassed looks on my parents faces, another woman stood up for my family and told that ignorant woman to leave my family alone. My dad thanked the woman and then after we finished eating, we paid the bill and left. I felt bad for embarrassing my parents but they told me not to worry about it.

For me being at home was a lot easier than being in public, because at home I had the same routine, which gave me the structure I needed at the time to get through my day.

My favorite part about being at home was when I would spend hours outside just running around and playing pretend. Being outside was awesome because when I was outside; I could be around the trees and breathe in the sweet scent of nature and fresh air. When I was outside it made it easy for me to go into my world and visit with my imaginary friend Aries.

Aries was the best she was always there for me and helped me understand my wild and sometimes crazy imagination. Together we would fight dragons, climb up to the treetops of trees, and tickle the sun and sky. I loved being outside and playing around with and seeing what magical things would happen to us. Whenever I was afraid to go to sleep at night she would chase away all the scary monsters and bad dreams with her magic stardust. I felt that as long as I had Aries by my side nothing in the world could go wrong.

She was the kind of friend that you could tell anything to and she would not judge or betray my trust. She was also beautiful with long blonde sunlight colored hair and piercing blue sparkly eyes. I remember one night in particular I was having a hard time sleeping, since I did not want to play with my toys I called Aries. When she arrived, we went into the imaginary world and journeyed to the magical Jinglebellaton forest. As we were walking through the forest and taking in the sights, we danced with the magic dancing oak and maple trees that grew there.

As we were dancing three fierce, fire breathing dragons started to burn down the trees. Before they could do, any real damage Aries and I fought them away with magical water. Once the dragons were gone, Aries and I restored the trees and we continued dancing. We danced and danced until finally I felt tired enough to go back home and go to sleep. Even though Aries was a great friend, the most important people in my life were my family.

I loved my family and I was really close to them, we used to love doing special family things together like going to the beach or the movies. Unfortunately that did not get to happen as often as I would have liked, but I just made the most of the time we did get to spend together.

My father was in marketing and traveled all over the country for his job, and my mother was a Cardiac Cath lab nurse at a hospital in a nearby city. Since my father traveled a lot with his job, he was not always around to help my mom take care of my brother and me. While my father was out of town, my mother took care of everything, except when she was able to hire a babysitter to look after us. Not having my dad around was hard; we all missed him a lot, but he would call us every night, to see what was happening. We would love when he would call because it felt like he was right there with us and helped us not much miss him as much. He was a great father but I wished he had been around more often.

Since my parents both worked, my brother and I had many babysitters. The one babysitter that stuck out in my mind was Joanna. Joanna was a loser, and a real low life creep, she was cold hearted, smelled like rotten food and stole things from my parents. She had greasy and dirty brown hair and she always carried the scent of cigar smoke and alcohol. One night after she made us kids our dinner; she told me to eat better and called me a slob.

"Gracie you are such a slob, look at the mess you made."

"How many times do I have to tell you not to use your hands, use your spoon?"

"You're three years old for goodness sake you should know how to use a spoon now.

"Well what have you got to say for yourself young lady."

After hearing her say this, I decided I was going to get revenge. I had put up with her disrespectful actions and comments for months. I was tired of putting up with her disrespectful comments so I took matters into my own hands. She had on a white shirt and asked me what I thought of it, I thought to myself here is my big chance. I took my bowl with macaroni and meat sauce and threw it at her. When it landed, there was macaroni and sauce all over her shirt and her hair. I know I probably should have felt bad about doing something so rude and disrespectful but I did not. She had it coming and deserved what she got.

"Bullseye!"

"Oh yuck, great just great, I have macaroni and meat sauce all over me"

"What did you do you little brat?"

"Look at what you did to my shirt and my hair."

"Wait till I tell your mother what you have done."

I know what you are thinking diary and people reading this diary, I should not have done that. It was rude and disrespectful but what you have to understand is she had pushed me too far. After she stormed out of the room, my brother and I started laughing because I did not feel the least bit bad or the least bit sorry. She had it coming she had been making our lives miserable so I gave her a taste of her own medicine and it felt great.

    When my mother came home, she kissed my brother and me and then Joanna appeared with an angry look on her repulsive face. After speaking with Joanna, my mom was stunned and shocked by my behavior because I had never done anything like that before. After collecting her pay Joanna left and my mom while trying not to laugh told me throwing my food at Joanna was not polite and not do it again. After that, she asked me what caused me to throw it, and I told her she called me a slob, and that made me wrathful. She told me she understood but regardless of what Joanna did, she was an adult I was a child and I had to respect her.

    I did not like having to respect Joanna but I also knew better to argue with my mom. After giving it, some thought, I decided I would treat Joanna with respect, and hope that she would do the same in return. A few months went by and things were getting better or at least I thought they were getting better.

    One hot sunny day Joanna left my brother and me alone in her convertible with the keys in the ignition. Everything was going fine until, my brother accidently bumped something and the car rolled down the hill with us inside. As we were rolling down the hill, I closed my eyes because I was apprehensive and I did not want to see what was going to happen next. The car hit a tree and glass from the windshield went all over the ground. I was terrified but I just closed my eyes and hoped it would all be over soon.

Fortunately, we both survived with only a few injuries thanks to the quick thinking of one of our neighbors who saw what had happened and called 911. Even though we were not severely hurt the paramedics, took us to the hospital to make sure we were okay. We went to a children's hospital, and not long after we arrived the paramedics wheeled us into a room, and our parents arrived.

A few minutes after that Joanna showed her face, and my parents let her have it. They told her they were firing her not just for the accident but also for stealing thousands of dollars from my parents for weeks.

She tried to defend herself but my dad told her not to bother and that the police were already on their way to the hospital to arrest her. Once the police arrived, she ran towards the exit but was stopped, handcuffed and arrested. It felt satisfying to see that thieving, conniving bitch get what was coming to her. After the doctor cleared us to go home, our parents took us out for ice cream, and bought us each a new toy from the toy store for being so brave.

A few months went by, we went to court, and the judge found Joanna guilty of child endangerment and larceny. The judge sentenced her to thirty years in prison and she had to pay back my parents every penny that she stole from them. It was satisfying to see that repulsive troll receive what was coming to her, but even though Joanna was in jail my brother and I still worried about who was going to watch us next. We just hoped whoever it was they were better than

Joanna was and did not lie; steal or put us in potentially dangerous and deadly situations.

As the months went by, we went through a few other babysitters. They were not great at watching us but my parents were working and did not have a choice. They were the best parents my brother and I could ask for and they did the best they could to take care of us. My mom even considered having us move to another state so that we would be closer to my dad, and our grandparents could watch us but that plan did not work out.

Fortunately, for me my brother Jason took care of me and kept me safe. I loved spending time with Jason, and he was a great older brother. My brother was an athletic kid, with a muscular build and adorable big brown eyes. He also had a friendly personality that made many kids want to be his friend. However, he spent the majority of his time with me, because he knew I needed him. I loved spending time with him and doing different activities together, such as basketball or soccer.

Jason was an amazing older brother and I loved him a lot, he was always there for me and took care of me. I loved playing with him; he was always kind and patient with me. He was also great at teaching me how to do things like ride a bike and how to make a fort out of a tree. Spending time with Jason was always a blast it did not matter what we did as long as we were together.

When Jason was around I felt safe, and that no, one could hurt me. Even though my brother was six and I was four he was my protector. I looked up to Jason and he always showed me the right way to do things. He was the best big brother I could have asked for even if he was a little bossy at times. I knew the reason he was bossy was he wanted me to be safe and have a good life.

Another babysitter we had was not as bad as Joanna was but she was still pretty awful. Her name was Carla Fishermant and unlike Joanna, she let us do whatever we wanted. However, she would only do that as long as we were quiet and did not interfere with what she was doing while she was supposed to be watching us. She was sixty years old with long grey hair, blue eyes, and always wore large circular framed silver glasses on a gold-plated chain. She also smelled like cigarette smoke and rotten cabbage.

While my brother was at school, I was alone with her and to be honest she scared me a little, because she dressed like a scary witch from a fairy tale book. She forbade me from going outside, so instead I watched boring TV shows and played with my toys in my room. I did not mind it too much because I had my dolls and stuffed animals to play with. However at times, I was bored and wished I had had someone to play with instead of always having to play by myself.

Sometimes I would play with Aries but it was not the same as having Jason to play with. I wished that I could make things better, and that Jason could be there for me. I was about to get my wish but things did not exactly go the way I hoped they would. One day instead of walking my brother to the bus stop, she told him he had the day off and she took us to her house. Her house was a beautiful historical Victorian with beautiful Maple trees in the front yard, and a pool, and a basketball court in the backyard.

We had a great time she called the school and told them my brother was sick so that they would not call my parents. To ensure that we would not tell our parents what had happened Carla bribed us with homemade chocolate chip and peanut butter cookies. The cookies were yummy but I still wish we had told our parents, because if we had what happened the next day would not have happened.

The next day my brother actually did have a day off from school so my mom took us to Carla's house. When we arrived at Carla's, she said hi to my mom and then my mom kissed us goodbye and headed off to work. After my mom, left Carla told us to go play in the den while she made a few phone calls and checked her email. Since we did not want to get in trouble, we decided to read some books and act out the stories. While we were acting out the stories, she came out and said we were going to the local grocery store to buy milk and juice.

We got in her car and were quiet as mice because when we were not quiet she would yell at us. As we drove to the grocery store, I could feel my heart pounding, but I did my best to ignore it and just tried to make the best of the situation. When we arrived at the store she told us to stay in the car, and she would be right back.

The problem was she left the windows closed and since she took the keys with her, we did not have air conditioning. It was hot outside and as the minutes passed I felt like I was going to die. Fortunately, as luck would have it, a large muscular man wearing a police uniform came up to the car, broke the window and got us out of the minivan. While the first police office was trying to help us, other people were staring and trying to get a closer look at what was going on. Thankfully, another officer did a great job-keeping people away so that the other officer could give us the help we needed.

"Come on folks just move aside and let us help these kids."
"Officer are those kids going to be okay?"
"They are going to be fine now please go back to your business and let us help them."

After the officer got us, out we thanked him and I hid behind my brother. Sensing I was a little afraid, he knelt down on one knee and asked my brother why he was not in school. My brother told the officer that our babysitter said he had the day off. He then asked us for a number to reach our parents. Unfortunately, we did not know our mother's work number by heart and our father was away on one of his long business trips. After pacing back and forth for a few minutes Jason remembered our mothers name and the hospital and department our mother worked at.

After giving the police officer the information, he told us to get into his car and wait for him. I was afraid but Jason grabbed my hand and I felt better. The police officer called the hospital, asked to speak to our mother and drove us to her work. As we were driving along he put the siren on, which caused my brother and me to laugh because we had never ridden in a police car before.

When we reached the hospital, the officer gave each of

us a plastic police badge. When we arrived at the hospital entrance, our mother was waiting for us at the lobby. When we saw her, my brother and I ran into her arms. After hugging my brother and me and thanking the police officer, she took us to the back room. Her boss let us stay there and one of the doctors stayed with us. Once he knew we were safe, the police officer left. As for Carla, she received jail time for child endangerment and neglect and my parents fired her. I was relieved that she was not going to be able to hurt us anymore but I still felt sorry for her. She was not a bad person exactly she just made a bad choice.

However, after I thought about it for a few minutes, I realized that she was an adult. An adult should have known better. She should have known better then to leave us in a car on a hot day, without cracking a window open. Later on that night, my parents apologized to us for leaving us with such an irresponsible babysitter.

We forgave them because we knew out parents loved us and would never do anything to hurt us on purpose. I told my parents I thought they were the greatest parents in the world, because even though they had busy lives they still always had time for the two most important people in their lives my brother and me. They were always there for us, no matter how tired they were or stressed they always made sure that my brother and I had everything we needed.

As I went to bed that night I hoped that, the next person they hired to watch my brother and I would make sure that we were safe at all times. I actually asked Aries what her thoughts were on the situation. However, she told me that I should not worry it was my parents' problem and they would come up with a solution. I just had to be patient and see what it would be.

Months went by and since my parents had not found someone they trusted to watch us, my father asked his mother to come and stay with us. When my parents told us that our grandma was coming to live with us for a while, my brother and I were excited to see her and spend some quality time with her. We did not get to see her very often, because we lived in Rhode Island and she lived in New Jersey. She agreed to come for a little while to see how it would work out.

I was so thrilled I could not wait to spend time with her and play games with her. I loved my grandma she was sweet and kind and loved us a lot, plus she would always make us cookies and other baked goods. Having my grandma around was interesting to say the least. She would bake brownies and other baked goods, and the best part was she always let me help her. I also loved the smell of her perfume it smelled like cinnamon and sugar cookies. Spending time with my grandma was amazing and special to me.

My grandmother was a pretty woman she had a kind and loving face with gray silvery hair and a warm smile. The days always seemed to go by a whole lot quicker when my grandma was watching us. Even if she was always losing her sets of knitting needles and did not know how to use the microwave, she was still a great babysitter. When she would lose a set of knitting needles, she made into a game whomever found the pair of needles would win a prize. When my grandma was around I felt safe and I knew nothing bad was going to happen. I knew my grandma would never do anything to put us in danger.

One of my favorite things to do with my grandma was reading books with her. Even though I was still learning how to read, she was always patient and would help me pronounce the words that gave me a hard time. However, it was not all fun and games there were issues that occurred when she lived with us. One night my mom was making dinner and my grandma went to open the refrigerator to get a drink. When she reached for the milk, she accidently bumped the container of blueberries, which caused all the blueberries to spill on to the kitchen floor.

"Great just great I just finished cleaning up the floor and now there is a huge mess to clean up."

"I'm sorry I will clean it up."

"No that's okay you have done enough."

"You know what, why don't you go help the kids wash up for supper while I clean up and then we will have dinner."

"Okay I will and again I'm sorry about the blueberries."

After apologizing to my mother, again my grandma helped my brother and I wash up for supper. After my mother cleaned up the blueberries, we had dinner. While we were eating, the table was silent which was not normal for us. Usually we told jokes and talked about our days.

I think my mom was still a little too angry with my grandmother for not putting the blueberries away properly. I cannot say I blamed her those blueberries made a big mess and not to mention it was a waste of perfectly good fruit. Eventually my brother broke the silence by telling everyone about what he had learned in school that day. I loved hearing about Jason's school and could not wait until it was my turn to go to school too. After we had had dinner, my dad called, he spoke to everyone and then he spoke with me. I loved our nightly chats because it was hard not having my father around. As usual, I told him all about my day, how much I missed him and that I wanted him to come home soon.

He laughed and told me he would be coming home that Friday and would be bringing home a surprise for each of us. I also told him about the blueberries and he told me my mom had already told him all about it. Eventually I had to hang up because my mom said it was time for me to take my bath and get ready for bed. I had a long and fun day playing outside with my brother and my grandma.

The moon was in the sky and the sun had said goodbye. After watching the sun set, I did my getting ready for bed routine. I knew that my least favorite part of the day was coming near. I was watching a home movie and put up a fuss about going to bed but my mom did not give into my tantrum. After I said goodnight to my grandma, she picked me up and carried me up to my room.

After we reached my room, I got into my bed, laid down on my green flannel sheets and looked around my bedroom. I saw my storybooks on the shelves, my dolls named Lucy Tiffany, Mary, Louisa and Isabell, my stuffed dogs and tigers Huffy, Tickles, Tiggy and Lucky my stuffed bears Mr. Cuddles, Fuzzy, Radar, and Ms. Snuggles and my

pink and white toy box, which had the rest of my toys. As I was looking around my room, my mom said to me
"See even your toys are going to sleep."
"Mommy toys don't sleep they just sit there and pretend to go to sleep.
"You're right Gracie they don't but if you don't get some sleep, you won't have any energy to play tomorrow."
"Can Huffy, Tickles and Tiggy sleep with me tonight?"
"Alright here you go now let's pick a story to read."
"Did I hear that you are reading a story?
"Hey, Jason, you are just in time come in and let's pick a story."

After reading, my mom and Jason left the room and I tried to close my eyes but I could not fall asleep. After thinking about this issue for a few minutes I thought to myself as long as I was quiet, I could play with my dolls and have a tea party. I tip toed out of bed, grabbed Lucy, Tiffany, Mary, Louisa and Isabelle and had a quiet tea party. I was having a lot of fun and I imagined that my dolls were too. I was also imagining we were drinking tea and enjoying fresh out of the oven chocolate chip and peanut butter cookies. Eventually I had to stop playing because I heard my mom.

Before she reached my room, I quickly got back into my bed and closed my eyes. After a few minutes had gone by my mom came in to see if I was asleep. When she saw that I was sleeping she gave me a pat on top of my head and started to leave my room, that is until she saw the messy state of my room. She put my dolls in my toy chest, placed my stuffed animals back on the shelf and walked out of the room. As soon as she closed my door, I grabbed my dolls and had another tea party. After I finished playing, I put my toys away and closed my eyes.

On that Friday when my dad finally came home, he handed each of us a surprise. I received an oak stained music box that played a soothing lullaby, my mom received a jade necklace, my grandma got a scarf and my brother got a new toy truck. We all thanked my dad for our presents and then we told him about all the wonderful things we had been doing while he had been away.

It was great having my dad home but sadly, it did not last eventually my dad had to travel again. The next few months were hard; my father was traveling and my grandma had to go back to New Jersey to take care of my grandfather who had become ill. Since my parents did not find a trustworthy babysitter, my mom had to figure everything out.

Sometimes she would take me to work with her after dropping my brother off at school, and I would stay in the back room and draw pictures for my mom to hang on her wall in her office. Eventually my mom found an affordable day care that was willing to take me until my mom could pick me up. I loved daycare, everyone was nice there, and there were many nice toys to play with. I also made some new friends that I would hang out with every day named Francine Polerson and Wanda Watcherson. We loved to play with the plastic ponies and play dress up with the different costumes that we found in the closet.

Another thing that came up while my father was

traveling were the different evaluations that my mother had done on me to help figure out what was going on with me because even though I had friends I was still struggling with a lot of things. I did not mind the evaluations much, most of the time the people were nice and would just ask different questions and have me do various tasks.

    After we received the results from the evaluations, it became clear to my mother that I was not like most children my age. My dad would call and my mother would fill him in and eventually they found out I had autism. Later that night my parents had a discussion in their room about what to do and how they were going to help me. While my mother was calm, my father was pacing back and forth. I am not sure why but it was probably because at the time my parents didn't know much about autism and how best to help me so that I could still go to a regular school and do everything that other children could do.

"Well at least we know what she has now.

"Yeah but honey neither one of us know anything about Asperger's Syndrome so how are we going to help our daughter?"

"We can do research and get her the best help available I am not going to have our daughter fall through the cracks."

"She is going to be successful I don't care what it takes we are going to do everything in our power to make her successful."

"Should we tell Gracie what she has?

"No she is too young to understand right now, it would be better if we wait until she gets older. "When she is older she will be more mature and can understand what she has a little better." Looking back on this I wish they had told me sooner but we will get into that later on in the story.

Now that I have told you, what happened before I started school let us get into what happened when I started school. When I was old enough to attend preschool, I went to the local preschool in town that was a small part of a large white church. When I first arrived at Springville Nursery school I thought the teachers seemed nice and so did the kids, and supposedly, it was the best preschool in town. It was great for the first few days and then the teachers' true colors emerged. Every day when my mother would drop me off, while the other kids played I had to go sit in a corner away from the rest of the class.

When I asked why one of the teachers Mrs. Bagperson told me it was because I was too weird and different and she had to "protect" the other kids. Therefore, while the other kids played with toys. I sat in the corner, doing the same rainbow puzzle, and colored alone all day long. When my parents found out what was going on, they pulled me out of school. After touring a few schools, they placed me at Stormville academy in Providence.

Within a few weeks at Stormville, I was content, and thriving as a student and as a human being. As the weeks went on, I made new friends and started to realize that I loved school. I had it all awesome friends and amazing teachers that accepted me just the way I was. They also gave me a special job so I would not cry when my mother would leave to go to work. Every morning my mom would take me to school and then she would head to work. After my mom left, I went to the room with little kids that were too young for the preschool.

While I was there, I would play with them and tell them made up stories about castles and fairy princesses and knights. After a while, Miss Casey would come get me and take me back to my classroom. After I walked in the classroom, I would spend the day hanging out with my friends on the playground, learning how to count, learning my ABCs, hearing new stories and taking naps at naptime.

Eventually it was time for me to move on and go to kindergarten. When it came time to graduate from preschool I was excited to see what was going to come next. I went to two different kindergartens one in the morning and one in the afternoon. I loved both my kindergarten classes and learning new things every day. I had friends at both schools and I got along well with my teachers.

At Lake elementary, I had Mrs. Washer; she was nice with a kind face and curly brown hair. She pushed me every day and made learning fun. My other teacher was Mrs. Green she had blonde straight hair and she was nice and kind. They worked with me every day to make sure I did not fall behind. I was successful in their classes because they did not give up on me. I loved going to their classes and hanging out with my friends.

Being at school was a lot of fun for me and I enjoyed hanging out with friends and learning new things every day. I felt that every day there was something new to learn and see nothing seemed impossible to me. I loved being at school, I never wanted to leave because I was always having a lot of fun.

I remember one day at Lake Elementary; I was out at the playground running around with my friends Alexis who was short with dark brownish blackish hair, and Lisa who was also short but had blonde curly hair. We were having a great time until two older kids began chasing us. We ran around and tried to hide but they found us and we continued to run around screaming and laughing. We thought it was just a game and at first, the game was fun.

It was fun until one of the girls shoved me onto the ground. I picked myself up dusted myself off and kept running as fast as I could. I was not sure why these older kids were chasing us but I was not about to waste time finding out. Instead, I tried to figure out a safe place for my friends and me to hide.

"Come on guys hurry up we have to hide they are after us, we need to find somewhere safe to hide."

"We can always hide underneath the bouncy bridge its safe there and they won't be able to get us."

Without another moment of hesitation, we ran as fast as we could to the bouncy bridge. We ran so fast I could hear our shoes hitting the ground as we ran. As we were running, my heart was pound in my chest and I could hear it my ears. When we arrived at the bouncy bridge, we crawled underneath it and tried to stay as quiet as possible. While we were hiding, my heart was still pounding in my chest, and Lisa was crying. I started to try to get her to stop but it was too late one of the girls looked under the bridge and spotted us.

"Come on girls what are you chicken?"

"Quit hiding and come on out and face the music."

Since we wanted to prove we were not chicken, we got out from under the bridge and ran away from the girls until Alexis, and I fell down. We scraped our knees and elbows Lisa helped us up and took us to the nurse. The girls tried to follow us but when we reached the nurses office, she told them to buzz off so they left. I guess they were afraid of the school nurse, which caused me to laugh and forget about my injuries.

After cleaning our scrapes, she put bandages on, and told us to go back to class. We thanked her for her help and we headed back to our classroom. After we got back to the classroom, it was time for our fifth-grade friends to come and do arts and crafts with us. As usual, the fifth graders came to the classroom that is all but one of them.

My fifth-grade friend Jessie was missing, there were other fifth graders there but I did not know them all that well. As they walked into the classroom and sat down with my classmates, I started to feel apprehensive and shy. Since I did not want to make a scene, I did what felt natural to me. I hid under the piano bench, which is where I always hid when I was feeling nervous and anxious. Once I was under the bench, I hugged my knees and stayed quiet and small. As the minutes passed, I hoped that if I stayed quiet and small no one would know I was there.

My teacher saw I was under there but instead of demanding I come out, she let me stay there. One thing I loved about Mrs. Washer was that she understood that sometimes I felt anxious about new people and new situations. Instead of scolding me, Mrs. Washer figured out that it was best for me to go somewhere where I felt safe. I stayed under the bench for a while until this nice girl named Amy Gacerson approached the piano bench, saw I was down there and extended her hand to me. Since I realized it was ridiculous and foolish to hide under the bench I grabbed her hand, and she slowly pulled me out from underneath the bench.

After I dusted myself off, she led me over to an empty table and offered to do arts and crafts with me. While we were doing arts and crafts, I asked Amy if she had seen Jessie that day and she told me that Jessie was sick. Since we wanted to cheer Jessie up, Amy and I made get well cards for her. After we finished making the cards, Amy promised that she would take them to Jessie at the end of the day since they lived in the same neighborhood.

The next day I was hanging out on the playground with my friends and Annie a fifth-grade bully started chasing us. We ran as fast as we could but we could find a safe place to hide. I thought for sure we were going to get beat up, but then Amy and Jessie came running over and told Annie to leave us alone. I was thrilled to see Jessie, and glad that she was feeling better. Eventually Annie left us alone and we thanked Amy and Jessie for standing up for us.

They smiled and offered to push us on the swings. I loved the swings and as we were swinging, I felt like we were flying through the air with the birds. I closed my eyes and pretended that I was a bird soaring through the sky. It was fun pretending to be a bird but I knew that eventually I would have to get back to reality. Eventually I opened my eyes, stopped pumping my legs, and dragged them against the sand so that I could get off the swing safely. After we got off the swings, Jessie thanked me for the card I made for her and then we decided to play tag. I was having such a good time I did not want recess to end. Recess seemed to be the one time of day I could just be myself without worrying about embarrassing myself.

    I could have stayed outside for the rest of the day, but unfortunately, that was against the rules. When it was time to go back inside, I was disappointed but Amy and Jessie said we could play together another time. Back in the classroom, it was time for arts and crafts. I made a picture frame and I planned to give it to my mom as a present. However, since Mrs. Washer liked it, so much I gave it to her instead. After arts and crafts, it was snack time and then nap time. I did not like naptime because I could never fall asleep and by the time I did, it was time to wake up again. I was content at school, I loved my friends, teachers and my routine, every day was the same and I loved the stability however all of that was about to change.

    One day after school, my parents sat me down for a chat. When I saw the looks on their faces, I knew I was not going to be happy about whatever it was they had to say. I took a deep breath and decided to hear what they had to say. What I did not know at the time was that what they were about to say was going to change my life forever.

"Honey we have to tell you something and you are probably not going to like it."

"After kindergarten is over you are going to have to switch schools again."

"What that is so unfair I can't believe what I'm hearing."

I stood up started pacing back and forth and tried to calm down.

"Why do I have to change school again when I am perfectly happy with the arrangement I have now?"

"Honey since we don't live in the bus route for Lake Elementary you are going to have to go to Willow."

"Besides your brother goes to Willow and he likes it. Don't you want to be with Jason next year?"

"Not if it means having to leave all my friends behind and be forced to go to another new school."

"I won't know anyone there besides Jason; I will be the outcast loner kid all over again."

"Honey don't you think you are being a little over dramatic?"

After hearing, my mother say that I got really upset and angry. A part of me wanted to ask how I was supposed to react to this news. I also felt like asking why they just suddenly decide to place me in a different school without even consulting me first. After fighting with my parents about going to Willow Elementary the following year I got up, went upstairs and slammed my bedroom door.

I did not want to go to Willow Elementary School but I knew I did not have a choice. The next day at school, I had to tell my friends next year we were going to be going to different schools. When I found them I walked up to them took a deep breath and told them the bad news.

"Hey Alexis Hey Lisa"

"Hey Gracie, what wrong why do you look like you just lost your best friends?"

"I have to tell you guys something and you are probably not going to be happy when I do."

"Oh okay well just spit it out and tell us it can't be that bad."

"I have to go to Willow Elementary instead of staying here at Lake Elementary with you."

"Oh no you're kidding me right?"

"I wish I was, I can't believe my parents are doing this to me." Lisa looked at me and put a gentle hand on my shoulder and said

"I know this seems like the end of the world but maybe going to Willow Elementary won't be so bad."

"We are really going to miss you but we will keep in touch and hang out outside of school."

"It'll be like we were never really apart."

    I laughed and after I took a step back and thought about it Lisa was right this was not the end of the world. I felt loads better after telling them and decided that whatever happened at Willow I was going to try to make it work. After kindergarten, I started to wonder what my new school was going to be like and if I was going to make any friends. I was going to have to face some challenges but I knew I could get through it. During the summer, my mother and I practiced my reading, writing and mathematics skills so that I would be able to keep up with the rest of my class.

On the first day of school, I was nervous and wished I was back at my old school where everything was safe and familiar. I missed my friends, my old classroom and even the playground. Willow felt like a strange and foreign place and I was sure I did not belong there at all. As the day went on, I wished I were anywhere but there, but decided to make the best of it.

When it was time to go inside the classroom I stood where the other kids were standing and tried to stay small. My teacher Miss Jones called out our names and as she called out our names, she told us which desk to sit at. When she got to my name, I sat at my desk and put my school supplies inside it and did not say a word to anyone. As I looked around my classroom, I felt really out of place and nervous.

As the day went on, I did my schoolwork and followed all of Miss. Jones instructions. At recess, I just sat on a swing and tried not to cry. I did not bother playing with the other kids because I did not like any of them. They all looked snotty and stuck up; I could not believe my parents did this to me. I told myself that when I got home I was going to give my parents an earful. I did not belong here I belonged back at my old school where everything was familiar and more fun.

As I was swinging on the swing set, I thought about my old friends. I wondered what they were doing and if they missed me as much, as I missed them. As I was thinking about them tears started to fall and streak down my face, but I wiped them away. I did not want to let anyone see me cry because I did not want to show that I was vulnerable, or for anyone to think I was weak.

    When the school day ended, I got on the bus and looked out the window. I did not talk to anyone I just sat and looked out the window the whole way home. I could not wait to get home and go to my room, and just cry and scream about this completely awful situation. When the bus stopped at my house, my brother and I got off the bus and ran to the house. When our mom let us in she asked us how school was and we both said fine and then Jason went upstairs to his room to do his homework and I went upstairs to do the same. Once my homework was complete, I played games on my computer.

    I was so miserable and wrathful at dinner that night that I did not speak to anyone. Even though I had wanted to give my parents an earful, I could not think of any words that would express how steamed and wrathful I was at them. Instead of talking and joking around, I just sat at the table and ate my food. After dinner, I cleaned up and went upstairs to take my bath and get ready for bed. After my bath, I went to bed, without saying a word to anyone. My mom came in but I pretended to be asleep so I did not have to talk to her. She tucked me in, kissed the top of my head, and left the room.

    Eventually I became more comfortable and used to being at Willow Elementary school. I met some nice kids and hung out with them at recess. I realized that even though she was nothing like my old teachers Miss Jones was a fantastic teacher. She did not care that I had a learning challenge. She was willing to help me as long as I put in the effort. As for my old friends that I had met before I came to Willow Elementary school, I still saw them almost every week.

We would hang out at each other's houses and it felt like we had never been apart. I also saw Alexis when our brothers had their Boy Scout meetings. I remember once we were having a Halloween party in an old rustic red barn, the party was a blast there was so much to do and see it was hard to decide what to do first. There was creepy Halloween themed music playing and cookies and all different kinds of candies on the desert table.

When the party was in full swing, Jason decided to scare me by jumping out from one of the hay bales. I screamed and laughed because it was funny. Even though I thought it was funny, I was determined to get back at him. I picked up some hay and threw it at him. However, instead of hitting him it hit my dad who started laughing. He brushed the hay off and told me not to do it again. The rest of the night was fun and we even went on a haunted hayride, which was more fun than scary. We also hung out with and rode the horses around the riding rings.

The horse I had was sweet and gentle named Misty she was a chestnut mare and did not go too fast. It was as if she seemed to realize that I was a little nervous. I could have stayed at the farm forever but unfortunately; I had to go home and get to bed because it was getting late.

The rest of that year went by fast and before I knew, it was time for me to start 2nd grade. Second grade was the worst year I had at Willow Elementary. My teacher Mrs.

Lemons was verbally abusive towards me almost every single day. At first, I thought she was nice and I liked her, and thought she was going to be a great teacher. However, as the weeks progressed I saw her true colors. I can still remember the first time she made fun of me in class.

It had been a long day already and at that time we were working on our spelling worksheet and I was struggling. Since I did not want to get a bad grade, I asked her for help, which is something I should not have done.
"Gracie how many times have I gone over these words with you?
"Are you so stupid and retarded that you can't even spell simple and basic words?"

I could not give her an answer that would satisfy her so I ran out of the room in tears instead. I ran until I found a bathroom and stayed there until the lunch bell rang. Every day was the same that year. Nothing I did was right or good enough for that old bat to deal with the abuse, I would bite myself whenever I felt melancholic or wrathful.

Eventually it got to the point where my principal decided she had to call my parents and set up a meeting with them. In the meeting, it came to my parents' attention that my teacher was making me feel like I was a waste of space, who did not deserve to be in her classroom. Once they figured out the truth suddenly things started to make sense to my parents. They told my principal and the others at the meeting when I would come home from school, I would be really angry and upset and they did not know why. When the truth finally came out my parents were furious. My principal assured them that she would be handling the situation and would speak to Mrs. Lemmons.

I felt relieved that I was going to get the help I needed but deep down I was still worried about Mrs. Lemmons. As the weeks went on Mrs. Lemons was still mean to me but I learned to ignore her and focus on my work. After a while, the comments she made did not really bother me that much. Whenever she was mean to me, I would think of some positive affirmations and say them in my head so that I would not get upset.

Once she realized I was not giving her the reaction she wanted, she did not know what to say. I was hoping that would be the end of my problems with her but it was not. On my birthday, she made fun of me and told me I was stupid and worthless. I ran out of the room and to the secretary's office, and asked Mrs. Williston the secretary to call my parents.
"Gracie calm down why do you want me to call your parents?"
"If you call my parents I can go home for the rest of the day, I hate this school and I hate Mrs. Lemmons."
"Gracie are you sure you really want me to call you parents?"
"I'm positive Mrs. Williston please call them and tell them to take me home.
"Okay well if you really want me to call them I will."
"Thank you."

When she called my parents, they came and asked me what was going on. When I told them my side of the story, they had a meeting with my principal Mrs. Connorsfield and me. After the meeting, my parents and Mrs. Connorsfields told me to go back to class and they would work everything out. After hearing from my parents and from me, Mrs. Connorsfields got Mrs. Lemmons and Mr. Bins the superintendent involved. After talking to Mrs. Lemmons and hearing complaints about Mrs. Lemmons from bunch of other parents, Mrs. Lemmons lost her job. Since all the other second grade classes were full, my class had a substitute teacher for the rest of the year.

The last few years I spent at Willow Elementary school were much better. I realized that Willow was a great school and I loved it there. I discovered school was not hard for me as long as I worked hard and gave one hundred percent effort. School became a place where I could be myself, as long as I followed the rules and worked hard. I no longer worried about not being smart enough or good enough, and I was able to grow and thrive, as a student and as a person.

Another interesting thing well maybe not interesting but something that helped me was I started seeing Dr. Williams a child psychologist who had a private practice in the city. Every week I would go with my mom to meet with her. I enjoyed the meetings because I could talk about whatever I wanted without the fear of rejection and judgment. Therapy helped me when I really needed someone other than my family and friends to talk to about whatever was on my mind.

She was a great therapist and I felt like I could really trust her and talk to her about anything and anyone. She used to love to hear me talk about my friends and the different games and activities we would do at recess. I also told her about how much I loved being at Willow Elementary, seeing all my friends every day, and learning new things with my friends. Every day there was a new challenge and a chance to grow and thrive as a person. My parents thought Dr. Williams was amazing, but I think they also were a little jealous because I went to Dr. Williams with my problems instead of them.

    A few times Dr. Williams came to my school to observe me in my classroom, which sometimes caused teasing but I tried not to let it bother me. When she would watch me, sometimes I wondered why she was there but I chose not to deal with it. She would just sit in the back of the room, take notes, and watch me as I interacted with my teacher and fellow classmates. Sometimes I would look at her and wonder what she was thinking and if she was going to talk to me about what she had observed. One day she sat me down for a talk.

"Gracie you seem to really love being at Willow."
"It is an amazing school and I love being there, but I know my time there is coming to an end really soon.
"To be honest I am dreading going off to middle school I am going to miss being at Willow so much."
"Everything will be different in middle school a new school new rules and new teachers."
"You're right it will be but it will also give you a chance to grow and thrive as a human being, you're growing up Gracie you can't stay eleven years old forever."
"I wish I could because right now growing up stinks."

"You might feel that way right now but I bet you any amount of money one day you will feel differently."

As much as I wanted to believe my therapist, a part of me had severe doubts. A new school, new rules and other things meant big changes and adjustments. However, I also knew that no matter what my new school would bring I would be ready. One thing that really helped was the knowledge that for once I was not the only one that was going to be new there. Other kids my age would be going through the same thing and for some reason that made me feel better. I was ready for whatever this new school brought but I did not know just how challenging and tough it was going to be.

A few months later, my days at Willow ended and it was time for me to go to middle school. I still did not want to go but I knew even though I wanted to stay it was time to move on. After all every child has to grow, up and accept life's changes no matter what. I still went to the hospital every week to see Dr. Williams. During school, I hung out with Alexis and Lisa and introduced them to some new friends named, Millie, Amy, Abby and Rose. I was happy to have friends, but I wished I were back at Willow because I was having a hard time adjusting to the new school and the new teachers.

Sixth grade was a nightmare for me because; I was on the teal team and I had classes with a few teachers that did not want me in their classrooms. The worst of all was Mr. Goldberg my science teacher. He verbally abused me almost every day to the point where I would refuse to go to school, because school became a very unsafe and threatening place. I always felt I could not be myself at school because Mr. Goldberg made me feel worthless. I would try to stay small but that did not work out. Being in Mr. Goldberg's class got so bad that sometimes I would have to squeeze a stress ball to get through it.

I remember one day in particular was the worst day of all. It was in the middle of the class period and Mr. Goldberg was handing back on our science test, and I got a C+ on the test. I was devastated because I had studied hard and I thought I was at least going to get a B.
"Gracie you are such a loser I don't know why you even bother coming to class."
"You are so stupid Gracie it makes me want to vomit."
"I come to class because I have to, and for your information you are so vile and venomous that it makes me want to vomit."

After I said that, I was so wrathful and hurt that I ran out of the classroom. He called after me but I did not stop, I ran all the way to the bathroom and hid in one of the stalls. As I sat there, I wondered why I had to go to a school where I was not wanted. I hated it at Wildman Middle School but I knew I was going to have to stick it out so I made the best of it. I stayed in the bathroom until the end of the class period and then I went to my art class. I loved my art class and my teacher Mrs. Gemstone was the best. She was generous, caring, and very patient with all her students. She made being at school a little easier for me to bear.

During class, we were working on our ceramic

sculptures that depicted the object in our life that best described us as a human being. Even though normally I was talkative and bubbly in class, that day I did not look up from my work. I did not want anyone to see my tear stained face or see how melancholy I was. Instead of feeling sorry for myself, I just sat there and worked on my ceramic sculpture of my stuffed dog Huffy. Mrs. Gemstone could see something was bothering me but decided to let me work in peace, which I really appreciated.

    At the end of the day, I got on the bus and went home. Once I got home, I went upstairs to my room, started my homework and pretended everything was hunky dory. When my mom got home from work, it was time for me to go see Dr. Williams. Since I didn't answer when she called out for me, my mom went upstairs to my room to tell me it was time to go.

    After I grabbed my things, my mom and I got in the car and we drove to Dr. Williams' office. I could not wait to get there so I could ask her for advice about what to do. Once we got to her office and checked in, Dr. Williams came to get me from her waiting room.

"Hi, Gracie, how are you today?"

"Hi Dr. Williams, I am okay but brace yourself because today I am going to share a secret with you that I haven't told anyone not even my parents."

"Alright go ahead, I am all ears."

"Before I tell you what it is you won't repeat what I say to my parents will you?"

"It depends on what it is Gracie if I feel like they should

know I am legally obligated to tell them.

"Okay well I am having a lot of trouble at school, because I don't fit in."

"Can you be a little more specific Gracie? What do you mean by you don't fit in, do you mean with the students?"

"No I fit in with the students, it's my teachers most of them hate me. Especially my science teacher."

"Every day he makes fun of me and today he told me I was so stupid it made him want to vomit."

"Gracie that is not okay, he is bullying you and I am going to have to tell your mom what's going on so she and your dad can get you the help you need right now."

 I was angry at first but then I was relieved, I thanked Dr. Williams for listening and for the rest of the session, I told her about my friends. The next day was the same I got in trouble for running out of class but I did not care. I kept telling myself that I was going to have to keep my head down and do what I had to do to survive.

 I hated school but having friends helped make it a little more pleasant. As the days went on, I tried my best to blend in and lay low. When Dr. Williams called my mom, she was furious and told her she would talk to me about it as soon as possible. When I got home from school, my mom sat me down with my dad and asked me what was going on. I told them everything and as I talked, my father got more and more angry.

 At first, I thought he was cross with me, but he assured me that he was cross with my science teacher. After a few minutes of awkward silence, my father got up from his chair and promised me that they would find the underlying cause of what was going on. After speaking to my parents, I realized that things might start to get better. Perhaps I would get through the year without any more issues or drama.

When I went to bed that night I made a wish on a star that things would work out. A few weeks later, my father called the school and asked for a meeting with Mr. Goldberg and the school administration. On the day of the meeting, Mr. Goldberg started the meeting by saying he did not know why I was so unhappy and melancholic at school. After all I seemed to be getting along with the other students, and I seemed to be a smart and engaging student. He also told my parents that he loved me and loved having me in the classroom. He said I was a role model student and he thought I was an extremely bright child with a lot to offer.

After hearing the bullshit, my ignorant science teacher was saying I rolled my eyes and glanced over at my parents. My mother looked like she wanted to slap him and my father looked like he was ready to strangle him. He started shifting in his seat and biting his lip, waiting patiently for the opportunity to give Mr. Goldberg a piece of his mind. As soon as Mr. Goldberg stopped running his mouth, my dad opened his mouth and my mother and I just sat back in awe at what he said.

"First of all let's cut this nonsense, you don't love our daughter. My wife and I love our daughter."

"We aren't asking you to love our daughter we are asking you to help her reach her full potential."

"Gracie is an intelligent kid she doesn't need you to talk

down to her she needs you to teach her."

After hearing what my dad had said so far, Mr. Goldberg looked like he was about to have a stroke. He tried to jump in and defend himself but my dad stopped him because he was not finished. For a split second, I felt sorry for Mr. Goldberg but it passed quickly. While my dad was telling off Mr. Goldberg, I was sitting there trying not to draw attention to myself.

"Mr. Goldberg you and I both know that you don't want Gracie in your classroom so why are you sitting there pretending that you do?"

"If Gracie told you that she's lying I am very nice to her in class, in fact she is my favorite student."

When I heard those words, it was a slap in the face. I could handle every other insult he threw at me but when he called me a liar that was the last straw. I stood up and asked if I could pipe in. My vice principal told me that she would be happy to hear what I had to say. I looked Mr. Goldberg straight in the eye and defended myself.

"I am not a liar you have made this year a never-ending source of pure hell for me."

"I hate it here and I wish I didn't have to come here every day."

"Every day I have to use a stress ball just to get through your class. I wish I was never placed on the teal team."

After that, I started to choke so I sat back down, took a few deep breaths, and waited for Mr. Goldberg to say what he needed to say.

"I didn't mean what I said the way you thought I meant it; I was only teasing you."

After hearing that I wanted to slug him and give him a black eye however, I knew that would only add fuel to the already burning fire so I tried to calm down instead. After taking a deep breath, I stood up, and thought about what I wanted to say.
"Let me get this straight you call telling a student that she is so stupid that it makes you want to vomit teasing?"
"I call it bullying and if you are bullying students then you should not be a teacher."

After a few minutes of letting me say what I needed to say, my mother jumped in.
"Do you know that Gracie knows that she is unwanted at this school?"
"Every morning I have to fight with Gracie to go to school, you have made this place a very unsafe place for her."
"It has gotten to the point where I am starting to wonder if maybe we should have Gracie homeschooled this year."
After hearing my mom say this the vice principal jumped in.
"I can assure you Mrs. Paris that that doesn't need to happen."
"I will be talking with Mr. Goldberg and see if we can prevent this issue from happening again."

I was grateful to my parents for standing up for me but I knew that it was still going to be a long year. The rest of that year went okay but I tried my best to deal with the bad days and appreciate the good days. Mr. Goldberg still treated me like crap but I learned to ignore him because he was not worth my time and energy. I did not tell the vice principal because I did not think she would really care and I was a little afraid of her.

Eventually I came up with ways that would help me get through the bad days without any crying or getting upset. Every day whenever Mr. Goldberg would make one of his snide remarks, I would just smile and think about candy and bunnies. For some odd reason that helped and I was able to not show emotion when he would try to make me feel worthless and inferior. Things improved for a while but the worst was yet to come.

When my twelfth birthday came around it was a bad day. It started out great with my mom surprising me with my favorite breakfast, blueberry waffles with strawberries and my dad gave me one present early my first cell phone. When I opened the green and pink birthday wrapping paper covered box, I cried. I was also shocked because my parents had informed me that I was not getting one until I was thirteen.

My dad told me he wanted it to be a surprise for my birthday. My father also told me it was only to be used to contact friends and family. He also told me not to use it during school hours except for emergencies. I was in a great mood until I went to first period class, which happened to be science. When class started, he collected our homework with his usual troll looking grin and ugly grey blue eyes. As he walked around the room I could see his terrible adult acne that made his face look like a demented pizza. After he collected the homework, he then began asking us review questions for the test; we were going to have the following week.

When he asked me, my review question I gave the wrong answer. If that was not bad enough after I answered, he preceded to laugh and make fun of me.

"Once again Gracie has shown us how stupid and retarded she is."

"Gracie quick question how did you make it to the sixth grade when you're as dumb as a rock?"

That did it I finally snapped I was not going to take crap from this imbecile anymore.

"You know what, why don't you just shut the hell up. I might struggle with science but I am doing the best I can."

"You are such a pathetic jerk, you know what I am not going to waste anymore of your time I'm out of here."

After speaking my mind, I quickly gathered up my books, and ran out of the room. He called after me but I did not slow down or turn around instead, I ran out the door and out of school. I started crying my eyes out and shaking like a leaf. Since I was too scared to go back inside, I went through my purse, found my cellphone and called my dad. I told him I was not feeling well and he came to get me.

When he got there and saw how upset I was, he realized I was not sick but something had happened. When I told him what it was he signed me out for the day and took me to a local ice cream shop for an ice cream sundae. Normally he would not have done that but I think he knew I needed a break. While we were in the car, he told me everything was going to be okay, and that he would be speaking to my science teacher the following day.

After we had our ice cream, my dad took me to the park and we walked around for a while. After a few hours he took me home, and my mother and brother were there waiting for us. When my mother asked where we had been my father told her he had taken me out for a birthday ice cream and some father- daughter bonding.

She laughed and told us to go wash up for supper. After dinner, I opened the rest of my birthday presents, and then it was time for cake. It was my favorite marble with green, purple, blue, and pink tie-dye frosting. As I blew out my candles, I wished for strength to help me get through the rest of my school year in one piece.

The next day my dad was at my school and spoke to my science teacher. Miraculously by the time, I had science class Mr. Goldberg left me alone and did not make fun of me anymore. I still hated him and thought he was a venomous snake but at least I did not need my stress ball anymore.

By the end of the year, I was relieved the year was over and I prayed that the following year would be better. On the last day of school Mr. Goldberg tried to say goodbye to me but I just walked away I did not want to talk to him. As I walked out of school, I hoped that the following school year would be better.

The summer was a nice reprieve from school and I spent most of the days hanging out with my friends. I also spent time in Allentown Pennsylvania and Long Beach Island New Jersey visiting my grandparents. Even though summer was fun, I knew that eventually I was going to have to go back to school. However, for my own sake I was going to have to make it work and hope that things worked out. I was not sure what the new school year would bring but I just hoped it would be better than this year had been. I was also relieved that a new school year meant new teachers, which meant I would never have to see or deal with my asshole venomous science teacher again.

On the last night of summer vacation, I made a wish that my new teachers treated me with the same respect and dignity that I was going to show them. Seventh grade was awesome it was actually the best year I had in middle school. I loved my teachers and for the first time at my middle school, I was content and able to enjoy learning again. Every day was a new surprise and I really enjoyed that. I was finally on the right team with the right teachers. The ironic thing was even though green is my favorite color I had wanted to be on the silver team with my friends. I had also heard the green team was the worst team to be on, but it turned out to be the best thing for me.

Even though my friends were on a different team, I was doing really well and was happy and for the first time in middle school, I felt that I belonged there. My grades were excellent and I was having a blast. My parents were relieved that after such an awful experience in sixth grade, I was having a much easier experience in seventh grade. There was just one little problem, I was placed in resource math because I needed more attention and help than a single teacher could provide.

I loved being in resource math and my teachers Mrs.

Willsonfield and Mr. Cranberries were helpful and kind. However, when my parents found out my dad was furious. He told the school to put me in the regular math class because that was where I belonged I just needed to try harder.

    However my mom and the vice principal convinced him that the resource math class was a better fit for me. My vice principal told him this was the best solution at least until my math skills improved. I actually really liked being in that math class. The teachers were nice and I was able to get the attention and help I needed without having to feel like an idiot. Another good thing about being in the class was, my math grades improved drastically and so did my confidence.

    I also had a funny thing happen to me that year. It was the end of the day and as I was putting my things into my backpack to go home, I realized I could not find my English homework. Instead of panicking, I went to my English teacher Mrs. Banks and asked her if I could have another copy of the homework. She gladly gave it to me and then told me I had most likely missed my bus. I told her not to worry because I could call my mom on my cellphone and ask for a ride home.

    However I did not call my mom because I was embarrassed, I decided to walk home instead, which was a great idea except for two factors. It was raining outside, and I did not exactly know how to get to my house from school. Despite that fact, I decided I was going to have to figure it out. The weather was freezing outside but fortunately, I did not get too far. One of my teachers found me and told me to go back to the school. The bad news was the rain drenched my English homework but the good news was my Mrs. Banks handed me another copy. After a few minutes, one of the secretaries called my house to inform my parents so one or both of them could come take me home.

    A few minutes later my mother showed up, and boy did I get a lecture when I got in the car. She told me that walking home alone was dangerous and I was lucky that a teacher found me and not a sexual predator or something. I explained to her that I had lost my homework and I went to talk to my teacher about getting another copy. She laughed and patted me on the shoulder.

    After we got home, she said she was proud of me for doing the right thing and talking to my teacher, but next time she would rather have me call her or my dad for a ride home. After that incident, I decided it would be better if I kept my homework in a safer place so I would not lose it. My teachers were a great help and often helped me make sure I got to the bus on time.

    It was embarrassing but I understood that they were doing that because they did not want me to try to walk home again. I did a lot better academic wise then the year before but by the end of the year I was worried about what eighth grade would bring. When the school year ended, I decided to enjoy my summer and make the most of it. I hung out with my friends and my family and had a blast. Every day was fun and the summer was going by too fast. One the first day of school I decided to make this year the best year ever. I still hated the school and could not wait to leave but I was determined to make it work.

Eighth grade was probably the year I grew up and matured. My classes were great and I loved my teachers and got even better grades then the year before. Every day was a new challenge and I loved that. I loved rising up to new challenges, being able to show what I was capable of, and proving that I could handle my schoolwork.

However, it was not all smiles and rainbows there were some tough times but I got through them. The hardest thing to deal with was Marcus Fisherbinson constantly harassing my friends and me. One day he took the harassment too far and Mille kicked his ass. I still remember the day it happened. Millie and I were on our way to gym and all of a sudden, Millie heard Marcus say something.

The next thing I knew Millie ran up the stairs and they started fighting. After a few minutes, of them fighting on the stairs one of them bumped into me and I fell down the stairs. I hit my head on one of the steps and passed out. A few hours later, I woke up with a headache in the nurse's office.

The nurse gave me some medicine for my headache and then called my mom. My mom came and took me to the doctor because the nurse told her I might have a concussion. My mom rushed me to my doctor's office and the doctor said I was fine but to keep an eye on me. When we were in the car going home my mom asked me what happened. I told her that I lost my balance and fell down the stairs.

I did not want to tell her what really happened

because I did not want Millie to get in any more trouble than she was already in. Later on that night, Millie called me and apologized for causing me to fall.

    I told her not to worry about it, I was fine and I would see her in school the next day. The next day at school, I found out that Marcus received three weeks of detention for starting the fight and for throwing the first punch. Millie got off with just a warning because not only did Marcus admit to starting the fight, an unknown witness who saw the fight spoke up on Millie's behalf. For the next few weeks, Millie and I managed to keep a low profile and eventually the fight became old news.

    Things would take an unexpected turn at the end of that year. Alexis told us she was moving away to Allentown Pennsylvania. Millie, Lisa and I threw a goodbye party for her. We were the only ones who showed up but we had fun so that is all that matters. After the party, we had my parents drop us off at the mall. We thought some retail therapy would help us feel better. We also braced ourselves for the changes that were about to happen. I was a little scared, however; I did not show it because it would not make any difference. I knew that things were still going to play out the way they were going to play out.

    During the summer, I spent as much time with Alexis as I possibly could, until she moved. The day she moved was hard but we wished her luck and that was that. For the first time ever I was not going to be able to hang out with Alexis anymore. Eventually summer was over and high school began. High school was hard but I loved it more than middle school. There was one issue however, that caused many problems. I had a hard time with Mrs. Finnerson the secretary that worked in the main office. However, at the time I felt that it was my fault because I missed the bus a few times in 9th grade because I was not able to open my locker. She made fun of me a lot, until the vice principal told her to knock it off and leave me alone.

She also had a visit from my father who told her the same thing. After that, she was nicer to me and I made it to the bus every day. Another weird thing that happened was stupid ignorant boys in my math and English classes started sexually harassing me. I will talk about the sexual harassment first. I still remember the day it happened. I was in my math class and Chris Lakeson and Willison Pincherson came up to my desk. After standing there for a few seconds, they handed me a love letter that they claimed was from Winston Allensen.

When the bell rang, I went to my learning center class and I started to read the letter when I was supposed to be silent reading. When my case manager Mr. Williams caught me reading the letter instead of a novel, he asked me what it was. When I showed it to him, he asked me who wrote it I sighed and told him about the two boys who had given me the note in my math class.

He walked me down to the principal's office and had me speak to the principal about the note. After talking to me for a few minutes the principal Mr. West, called the number and it turned out to be the number for a shipping and receiving store in town. When I found out I started crying but the principal put his hand on my shoulder and tried to make me feel better. After two weeks of questioning Chris and Mark, they received a two-week suspension from school.

Since Winston Allenson had nothing to do with it he was not suspended, but he did apologize to me for his friends' behavior, which I thought was very benevolent and gallant of him. I told him it was fine; I was just grateful that the whole mess was finished. I was also grateful that I would be able to move on and focus on more pressing matters. After word had gotten out about the suspension, I was afraid to go to school but most people were supportive and kind. Many people congratulated me on sticking up for myself. It was nice to have so many people supporting me, but to be honest I was hoping that eventually I would be able to move on.

When my brother found out about what had been going on, he asked me if I wanted him to handle them when they returned to school. I told him no because I thought the suspension was punishment enough. I was also afraid of what my brother would do because he was very protective of me and I loved him however, sometimes I wished he had let me fight my own battles.

I guess all older siblings are like that, probably because they love their younger siblings and do not want to see them get hurt. He was my older brother and one of the most important people in my life but sometimes he took his job of defending me a bit too seriously. Fortunately, this time he let me handle it on my own and told me I handled it very maturely.

The rest of the year went by smoothly, and I ended up really loving school and doing really well, in my classes. My favorite class was Civics, which was a history and political class taught by Mr. Jacobs. Mr. Jacobs was a very nice and kind teacher willing to let us discuss any topic we wanted as long as it related to history.

He knew how to inspire a class and grab the students' attention. I did well in his class because I loved history. It also helped that I had American history drilled into my brain every summer by my mother. Mr. Jacobs understood my learning disability and taught me in a way that I felt respected. Feeling respected meant the world to me, because in middle school most teachers babied me except for a select few. While my classes were excellent, something happened in my social life that changed me in ways I never expected. Josh Fincherson whom was a friend of mine from middle school told me he really liked me.

We started dating and were dating for about three months when everything changed. My brother found out we were dating and told my parents. They were okay with it as long as I kept up with my schoolwork. Eventually we broke up because I caught him kissing another girl in the hallway. I was hurt at first but eventually I picked myself up, dusted myself off and realized he was not worth my time. I decided that for the time being I was going to focus on school.

That year I did really well academically, much better than I had the year before which made me feel proud. When it came time for the IEP meeting, the school psychologist told me I had Asperser's Syndrome. When I asked what it was, he told me it was a high functioning form of autism. I was so angry with my parents for not telling me. They had known all that time and not once bothered to tell me. I was so pissed off I thought smoke was going to come out of my ears. The whole care ride home I did not say a word, I was too aggravated to say anything to my parents.

When we got home from the meeting I was still angry, so I went to my bedroom closed the door and screamed into my pillow. After that, I decided to do some drawing which always helped me calm down after being angry with my parents. I also decided to go down to the basement and play with my toys for a while.

A few hours later, my parents called me back upstairs for dinner. Even though I was not hungry, I marched up the stairs and had dinner. During dinner, I did not have much to say to my parents or my brother I just sat there and ate my food. After dinner, my brother went out with friends and they tried to explain to me why they had not told me sooner.
"When did you find out what I had?"
"We found out when you were three years old. The doctors told us after the evaluations we had done on you were complete."
"I get not telling me when I was little but why didn't you tell me when I was ten or twelve?"
"You were still too young to handle this and we wanted to protect you."
"Basically what you are telling me is it was better for me to hear it from the snotty school psychologist, and be

blindsided then have you my own parents tell me?"

"No we…"

"Don't bother oh I can't believe this this sucks."

 After hearing everything, I had just heard I decided to go to my room and digest everything that happened. Everything had happened so fast I was so upset I could not even see straight. I just wanted to go to sleep so I did. When I woke up the next morning, I was still really aggravated, when I went downstairs I mumbled good morning to my mother, ate my breakfast and then my brother and I left for school. In the car, I did not talk to my brother at all when he drove us to school. Fortunately, he respected that and we just listened to the radio. Listening to the radio gave me the time and space I needed to process everything.

 It also gave me time to figure out how to make sure that I did my best to keep my learning difference from interfering with my day-to-day life and activities. During school I went to my classes like I usually did but I could not help but wonder if my teachers knew about my learning difference. If they did know what I had, why had no one ever bothered to tell me?

 How could they not realize how embarrassing it was for me to found out from a therapist that I did not know from a hole in the ground? At lunchtime, I went to the library and took out my laptop. I decided I should pretend to be working on homework so Ms. Ruderson the grouchy librarian would not kick me out. A few minutes went by and Millie found me, she was just staring at me as if she did not know what to say to me. I told her everything and she just sat there and listened.

"I wonder if there is a way to access my school records."

"There is you could get them through the office, but why do you want to look at your school records?"

"My school records might be able to tell me when I was diagnosed, and maybe some other stuff that my parents never bothered to tell me about."

Millie just sat there and stared at me as if I had a hole in my head.

"Gracie don't you think you are being a tad over dramatic about this whole thing?"

"Millie how would you feel if you found out that your parents were keeping this huge secret from you?"

"I would probably be cross and maybe even a little hurt.

"However, I would also try to understand that my parents were trying to do what they felt was right."

"I get that I really do but I can't help but feel as if my whole world has been turned upside down."

"What I mean is I'm not sure who I am anymore."

"Of course you know who you are you're Gracie Elizabeth Paris a smart bold, suborn, and determined young woman."

"Thanks Millie but I really want to do this I have to know; I have some many questions that need answers."

"Okay well if it is that important to you, after lunch you and I will go down to the office and solve this mystery once and for all."

After we ate our lunches, we went into the mail office and told Mrs. Finnerson we needed to look at my school file. "Millie why don't you go back to class, and we will help

Gracie."

After giving it, some thought Millie and I decided I should do this alone and she went back to class. I promised to call her and tell her everything I found out. Mrs. Finnerson gave me my file, under the condition that I read it and brought it back to them the next day. After I agreed to their condition, and she wrote a late pass for me and I went back to class.

When I got home from school, I went upstairs, did my homework, and read my file. Some of the things in it shocked me but it did not give me the information I was looking for. I was so frustrated that I did not feel like seeing or speaking to my brother or my parents. Later on that night, my mother called up to me to come downstairs for dinner. During dinner, I did not really talk much I did not have anything to say. I still felt furious that my parents had not told me. After dinner, I called Millie and told her that while my file did provide information it was not the information I was looking for.

"What's the next step now that you have seen your file?"

"I think I am just going to forget the whole thing return my file, and just make sure that I don't let my Asperger's stand in my way."

"Not going to lie Gracie I was kind of hoping that was what you were going to do."

I laughed and then after we talked about a few things and hung up. After talking to Millie, I felt a little better. The next day at school I returned my file and was about to leave when Ms. Finnerson said that the principal wanted to talk to me. I was feeling somewhat nervous because I had a strong feeling I was in big trouble. Instead of running way, which was my first instinct, I decided to just go talk to him and see what he wanted.

Ms. Finnerson walked me down to his office and knocked on the door. After he let me into the room, he told Ms. Finns she could go back to her work. Since I was still uncertain, what I was doing in the principal's office I decided to take a deep breath and just wait to see what he had to say. "Gracie I understand that you asked to see your school file yesterday is that correct?"

At first, I thought about lying to him but then I thought it would just be better to be honest.
"Yes sir I needed answers to some questions I had regarding my Asperger's Syndrome diagnosis, which up until two days ago I didn't even know I had."
"I am sorry if I violated any rules and I hope that Ms. Finnerson doesn't get fired, but I really needed to know."
"I understand Gracie this must have been confusing for you, and you aren't in trouble and neither is Ms. Finnerson.
"However, as your principal I feel I have to ask did you get the information you were looking for?"
"No I didn't, well I got some of the answers but the one big question that I had is still unanswered."
"Oh and what question is that?"
"When I was diagnosed and if that is why I get all the special services and privileges that I have had for so many years."
"Ah well unfortunately we cannot answer part of your question. That part of your question would be in a

psychologist or psychiatrist evaluation."

"However I can confirm that your Asperger's Syndrome is exactly why you have been getting special services."

"Oh well thanks, is it okay if I leave now?"

"Not quite yet, did you ask your parents about the questions you had, or even tell them you've seen your school file?"

When I heard his question, I thought I should lie and tell him of course my parents knew. I also knew it was wrong to lie so I just told him the truth.

"No I didn't tell my parents anything because I didn't think they would understand, and I don't feel comfortable explaining it to them."

"I think they would they're your parents and they love you."

"I want you to promise me when you get home you will talk to your parents."

"After all they just might surprise you and be able to help you through this."

"Oh okay but I still think it is a mistake but I promise."

"Okay then I will write you a pass for class off you go.

I went to class and as the day went on, I tried to picture how the conversation I was going to have to have with my parents was going to go. After I got home from school and I finished my homework I talked to my parents. I told them I was determined to succeed no matter how hard things got I was going to be successful, and I was not going to let anyone or anything stand in my way.

I also told them that even though I did not agree with their choice to wait until I was older to tell me what was going on, I understood why they waited. The rest of the year,

I made sure that I did everything in my power to make sure that I did not ever let this diagnosis beat me. During the summer, we went to Allentown Pennsylvania to visit my family.

The best part was when my Nanna took us to the brook. Being at the brook was amazing. Every time I would touch the weeping willows, smell the sweet-smelling flowers I felt at peace and happy. Spending time with my nana there was the best part of the trip to Allentown. The time passed slowly there, and every time we went, I enjoyed watching the different kinds of fish swimming in the water. Sometimes I would get really close to the water and be able to feel a slight cold mist as the water rushed pasted me.

When my sophomore year of high school came around it was an even better year than the year before. I met a teacher that by the end of the year became my favorite teacher. Her name was Mrs. Carson; she was tough but fair. I learned a lot from her, she really pushed me to do my best and to reach my full potential.

There were times I resented her for it but in the end, I understood why she did what she did. She and I worked really well together, after I stopped being such a smart ass and actually listened to what she was trying to say.

I also really liked my art teacher Miss Quinn. She was nice and I felt like I could talk to her about anything. I went through a tough time that year because my father was contemplating moving us to Massachusetts for a job opportunity. I did not want to move Rhode Island was my home I had lived there my whole life. All my friends lived there so if I moved I was going to have to make all new friends. Moving to Massachusetts was going to be tough but I knew I was going to have to make it work, because I loved my dad and I wanted him to be happy. His happiness meant the world to me. Therefore if moving to Massachusetts was going to make him happy then that was what we were going to do.

In order to help myself get through this rough patch; I took out my frustration on my artwork. After being concerned about me for a while, one-day Miss Quin asked me to stay behind after class. She asked me if everything was all right at home and I yes, and then I asked if I could go. My other teachers noticed a change in me too. I stopped talking and participating, so they called my parents and asked them if I was acting differently at home. My mother said that I was probably acting out because of the possible move to Massachusetts.

Fortunately, we did not end up moving and everything went back to normal. After a few weeks into the new school year, I decided to join the drama club and got the part of Jessie the singing and dancing mermaid. I loved it and I believe being in that play really helped me come out of my shell and show everyone what I could do. While in the drama club, I could show a side of myself that I did not show to anyone else because I felt free and safe there. I always looked forward to rehearsals, because the director knew how to get us as actors to give our best performance.

Even if our energy was down, he still made sure we gave him one hundred percent effort. His name was James

Ace and he knew what he wanted from his actors. One day we were doing the musical mermaid scene for about the tenth time because we were having a hard time getting the scene to flow. Jenna and I were Rosabell and Jessie two best friend mermaids. We did great we knew our lines and all the words to the song, and we had memorized the chorography to the dance. However, Andres and Zack who were playing Jack and Waldo the two male mermen were goofing off and not trying. Instead of getting frustrated, James told us to take five and get it together.

After five minutes the scene flowed beautifully, everyone said his or her lines and we made everyone laugh including ourselves. It was a nice stress reliever for me because I was struggling to figure out exactly whom I was and what I wanted to do. At rehearsal, I did not have to worry about being Jason's little sister, which was a label that I had carried my whole life. It drove me crazy because I wanted people to see me as me and not just as someone's younger sister. Whereas at the drama club I had my own identity which meant the world to me.

At the next few rehearsals, I nailed all my lines and all the dance moves to the different songs. Our dance coach Ms. Willisonville was impressed and told me to keep up the good work. As the weeks progressed, the rehearsals became longer and more stressful. However, it was all worth it because even though it was stressful I still had fun. Being in the drama club gave me an identity. Having my own identity with a perfect overachieving brother was priceless. My parents never compared us but other people did and I hated

it. I had teachers that would say
"Gracie why can't you be more like your brother?"

I always said, "We are not clones, we are two different individuals who happen to have the same parents."

I loved being Jason's sister but sometimes it would have been great if people just saw me as me and not as Jason's younger sister. Fortunately, the people that mattered saw me as me so that helped a lot, and I learned to ignore those who only saw me as Jason's sister.

However, being in the drama club was not all fun and games there was a lot of work that came along with it too. Since we could not afford to have professionals make the sets, we made them ourselves. I enjoyed painting the sets and seeing the play that we all worked so hard on come to life. Once they were finished, they looked amazing. After we admired the sets and all of our hard work, we did a run through of the play and it flowed perfectly.

At the end of the rehearsal, I was in awe of how far our play had come since we first started. I just hoped and prayed that the audience would love the play as much as we did. After rehearsal, I went home, did my homework, and had dinner. During dinner, my family kept asking about the play and I told them they would just have to wait and see, because I did not want to spoil it for them.

When it came time for the show in front of the whole school, I was really nervous but excited too. However, the day before the show I tripped over a table backstage and slammed my arm into one of the sets. Fortunately, it was not broken only bruised and I was able to perform in the big school show. After having me put some ice on it, James told us to run the scenes one more time.

The day of the show, I was trying my best to stay calm and keep my nerves down. I was doing a great job until it was time to get into my costume. After I put on my costume, I headed for backstage and felt like I was going to be sick.

After seeing how terrified I looked, my friend Jenna gave me a hug and told me I was going to be just fine. I took a deep breath and hoped she was right. When it came time to do my big scene, I said my lines perfectly without missing a single line or dance move. Despite not messing up my lines or dance moves, I did unfortunately lose my shoe.

My friend Jenna who was playing Rosabell and I were doing our beautiful duet and my flip-flop fell off right in the middle of the song and landed on the middle of the stage. I thought I was going to die of embarrassment. However, instead of getting upset about losing a shoe, I just kept going and hoped that no one noticed. After the scene was over we took our bows and the audience erupted with applause.

The applause was great but it was also a little overwhelming. For a split second, I felt a little woozy so I sat down until I felt able to stand back up again. I was so happy that the school loved the show. It felt like we were a bunch of rock stars that had just given an amazing concert. I was also happy because my brother and his friends had given us a standing ovation.

It felt good to make my brother proud of me. I was so happy and hyperactive my friends kept laughing and told me to calm down. I laughed and told them I could not help it. I was so joyful and proud of the cast and myself. We put on an amazing show and the school loved it.

After the show, I changed back into my normal clothes and went back to class. Throughout the remainder of the day people kept coming up to me and telling me what a great job I did. It was fantastic to have so many appreciative fans, but I was also feeling a little overwhelmed by all the attention. Most of it had come from people who usually did not notice me at all, because I was so shy and quiet.

After school was over for the day, I went to my locker and put my books in my backpack. As soon as I had everything I needed I headed to the bathroom to change into my opening scene costume for rehearsal. The costume I chose was a beautiful blue dress, a black bonnet with a pink feather and matching black platform dress shoes. Once I was in my costume, I headed to rehearsal.

At rehearsal, everyone was feeling unnerved and stressed out. Since James wanted us to relax, he had everyone gather around him and sat us down for a little talk. He had us close our eyes and take some deep breaths. He then told us to open our eyes and look at each other. As we did that, we all realized that we had worked hard on this play. We were going to do our best to make sure that this was the best play ever.

After the pep talk, we decided to do one more run through just to make sure that we knew all the lines and dance moves. After rehearsal, my dad picked me up and took me home. Later that night I practiced the dance moves in my room. I also practiced saying my lines in the mirror repeatedly so I would not forget them on stage during the performances.

When the big opening night came, my stomach was doing flip-flops all day. I was so nervous I could barely eat my lunch. I was afraid I would not be able to keep it down. Instead I just picked at it and then put my lunch back in my backpack when none of my friends were looking.

When the final bell rang at the end of the day, I was really feeling sick to my stomach and felt like I was going to throw up. I ran to the bathroom but did not throw up. I still felt sick but I took a deep breath and told myself to get a grip. Since I did not want to be late for rehearsal, I quickly changed into my costume and headed to the theater. At rehearsal, I felt even worse my stomach was doing backflips and my heart was pounding in my chest.

Once James got rehearsal started, he had us do a run through of the show so that he could see if everyone knew his or her lines and dance moves. Unfortunately, for me, I fainted during the opening scene. When I finally woke up, I was so embarrassed I wanted to sink into the floor.
"Gracie are you okay what happened?"
"I'm alright I think I was just feeling a little dizzy but I'm fine."
"Well alright if you are sure, everyone let's take it from the top."

At the end of rehearsal, I went home to do my homework and eat dinner. When it came time for me to go back to school, I was already in my costume I was still feeling nervous but I just took a few deep breaths and hoped the show would go on perfectly.

As I walked down the stairs, my dad took pictures. My brother told me to knock them dead, I smiled and then it was time for me to go. The two performances were amazing everyone did a great job and the audience loved it. On the third night of the performance, there was heartache. The boy I had had a crush on since seventh grade rejected me.

A few friends had told him I like him and demanded to know if he liked me. His name was Angelo Marris and he told them he liked me as a friend but that was it. I was so humiliated I cried. When it came time for the show to start, I gave my best performance then after the show, I went straight home.

When we got home, my mom made me macaroni and cheese with Jell-O for dinner. I know that sounds weird but it made me feel better. My parents knew something was wrong but decided not to press me on the matter.

After a while, I went to be and tried to sleep but just ended up tossing and turning. I kept thinking about Angelo and how I was going to face him at school. The next day at school was the worst day of my life all my friends were asking me what happened and I did not really want to talk about it.

During lunch, I hid in the library and worked on my homework. I loved working in the library because it was peaceful and quiet. After lunch, I went to class and I tried my best to focus and pay attention. As soon as the final bell rang, I went straight home, and went to my room so I could have some alone time.

When my mom got home, she called up the stairs that it was time for dinner. As soon as dinner was over, I went to the family room computer and started talking to my friends online. After a while, I did not want to talk to my friends anymore so I went upstairs to take a shower. After I got out of the shower and had gotten ready for bed, my mom came upstairs and told me that Millie was on the phone.

I talked to Millie and then I went back downstairs to use the computer. We talked about my birthday party, which was to take place the next day. I was turning sixteen and I was excited. My friends asked me what to bring, and I gave them a list. The next day my mom and I spent the day going grocery shopping for all the food I was going to need to have my party such as my birthday cake and of course my favorite thing pizza strips, in my opinion I couldn't have a birthday party without pizza strips.

We also moved the furniture around in the family room so that my friends and I would have plenty of room for our party. I was also driving her crazy because I kept asking how much longer until the party was going to start. Finally, after running around for the majority of the day, my party began and my friends started to arrive.

Once everyone was there, we set the room up for our sleepover and then it was time to have cake. When it came to make a wish, I knew exactly what to wish for when I blew out the candles. After we had cake, it was time to open my presents and have the dance portion of my party.

Everything was perfect and we were all having a great

time. I can still remember all of us in our pajamas dancing to the music, laughing and having fun. It was nice to hang out with everyone, being silly, and not caring what people thought of us.

After partying for several hours, we all decided to get some sleep. The next day we went shopping and after shopping for two or three hours we were hungry, so we went to the food court. We all consumed an excessive amount of sugar and started laughing randomly. Pretty much everyone in the food court was staring at us but we did not care.

The next few weeks flew by and before I knew it, it was time for the annual semi-formal dance. The semi-formal dance was the biggest event for the sophomore class. Everyone in our class was going and I was excited because I was going with my best man friend Angelo Marris. The not so fun part of going to the dance was trying to find a dress that fit and showed off my beauty.

To make sure I found the right dress my mother made me go to every dress shop in RI. We spent hours looking for the perfect dress until we wound up right back where we started. After several hours of trying on dress after dress, I found the perfect inexpensive bright lime green dress. While we were looking at all the beautiful prom stuff on display, I found the perfect shoes to match.

The night of the dance was perfect, and I had a great time with Angelo. He picked me up in a town car that he had rented for the two of us and brought me my favorite flowers pink roses. His dad drove us and we sat in the back, and I felt like a movie star on her way to the Oscars. When we entered the room, everyone was staring at us but we did not care we were two best friends hanging out together. We danced to every song, and when it was time to go home I was disappointed because I did not want the night to end.

The rest of that year flew by and the next thing I knew it was summertime. The next part of this story takes place during my junior year of high school. It seemed like any other day of my junior year of high school. That morning as usual I had done my morning routine. I said goodbye to my parents and got into my brother's car so he could take me to school. It was Friday my favorite day of the week, because it meant that as of 1:45pm my weekend could officially start.

The morning went by quickly enough and then it was time for lunch. As usual, I sat with Millie and we talked about boys and other teenage stuff. My day was going well but I was going through a rough time and needed to go to the guidance office for a little while. My Nana was sick with bone cancer and was getting worse. Over the weekend, she went to the hospital due to fluid getting into her lungs. I told Millie where I was going and headed out the door.

While I was at guidance speaking with one of the guidance counselors, Millie was getting the third degree from my controlling and sometimes violent friend Alan Winston. By the time I got back, Millie told me Alan was looking for me. When I heard that right away, I panicked because I knew he was probably furious. Millie asked me if I wanted to go for a walk, so we did and I hoped that we would not run into Alan on the way.

Most of the time Alan and I got along really well but

there was one major problem. He did not always respect that I needed to talk to someone besides him, when I was feeling angry, depressed or stressed. Actually, he was trying to control my life and would call me on the phone constantly. Sometimes he would call two-four times a night it drove my family crazy I had mixed feelings about it. On the one hand, it was nice having him to talk to but sometimes I needed my space.

I also did not appreciate him trying to tell me what to wear to school every day. Every time I thought about telling him off, he would look at me with those hot fudge chocolate brown eyes and I would melt. I did not have a crush on him exactly, but he was the kind of person that appeared to understand my situation and me. I trusted him, even though others including my parents did not think I should. He was an okay person most of the time. A part of me actually felt sorry for him because he did not appear to have many friends.

He would try to fit in with people but they did not always accept him. Millie and I walked aimlessly through the halls, before we knew it we ended up back in the lunchroom. We sat down at the table and I turned around and saw Alan glaring at Millie and me. He walked out of the lunchroom and I stupidly walked out too. Millie and our other friend Amy followed me out of the lunchroom.

I started to shake and my heart was pounding in my chest. Since I needed to calm down and catch my breath, I sat down next to the pay phone. Eventually I walked back into the lunchroom and Alan stopped Millie and Amy. He started yelling at them until Amy told him to back off. A few minutes later Millie and Amy went to guidance to try to calm down and speak to a guidance counselor about what had just happened.

After they went to guidance, they came back into the lunchroom and sat with me. Amy had her hands shaped into two tight fists and I could tell she was furious I was too but I was also shocked about what had just happed. As we were sitting at the table, I could feel my heart pounding inside my chest. After a few minutes, I felt like I could not breathe so I went back into the hall to try to catch my breath.

As I was trying to catch my breath, Alan showed up grabbed me and asked me what Amy said to me. When I would not tell him, he shoved me against the pay phone. I cried and he yelled at me to stop. I looked at his eyes and they looked like there was fire in them. I did not know what to say so I just stood there, crying my eyes out. I did not want to look upset when I went back to class so I wiped my face and my eyes. As I was trying to wipe my face and eyes, he continued to yell at me. After hearing, him yelling at me my friends looked over and rushed to my side.

Millie pulled me away from Alan and Amy told him to go away. After seeing the commotion my other friends Rose Willamon, Abby Zingerfeltson and Betty Beansonfield came over and tried to calm me down. While they were helping me calm down, he lunged at me. Millie sensing was going to happen jumped in front of me and he backed off. After what seemed like forever, we went back to the cafeteria and finished our lunches. After lunch, Amy walked with me back to class.

I was not sure where Millie went because I was in too much shock. Amy put her arm around me and we walked out of the cafeteria in silence. Abby, Rose and Betty walked behind us. As we walked I felt more and more shocked about what had just happened, but I did not have much time to dwell on it. After Millie, Rose and Betty went into their classroom, Abby Amy and I headed back to our Geography class. In our Geography class, our teacher Mr. Wilkinson told us to get into our project groups. We were supposed to draw and paint a small part of the United States and then discuss it in front of the class.

My group, which consisted of Amy, Abby and I had chosen to talk about and make a map of the western region of the United States. We had finished the outline of the map two days prior to that day so now it was time for us to paint it. However, my hand was shaking so hard, it was hard for me to hold the paintbrush to paint my part of the map. Fortunately, Amy was willing to do my half for me. Since Amy could not paint both her half and my half at the same time, Abby painted the rest of the map so that the work would be done faster. I felt bad I was not able to help but I was still pretty shaken up about what had happened during lunch. When Mr. Wilkinson noticed I was not painting the map, he asked me what was going on but I did not want to talk about it.

Actually, I was too shaken up and unnerved to talk about it. I just told him it had been a rough week and pulled out my Geography book and started looking up different facts about the western region of the United States. As I looked up each fact about the region, I wrote down the pages so I could type up the facts when I got home.

    While I was reading and writing down the page numbers, my friend Jane saw the look on my face and came over to ask me what happened. I told her everything I did not mean to, it just spilled out of my mouth. After spilling my guts to her, she told me I should report it to the principal. After Jane had gone back to her desk Amy scolded me and said, I should not have talked about it with people that were not there.

    For the rest of the class period my group focused on our map, which turned out pretty great, and I was sure we were going to get an A. After classes were over and the final bell rang, I went to my locker, grabbed the books I would need for my homework and headed outside to catch the bus. Even though it was a Friday and it was the weekend, I still felt upset. When I got home from school, I put my backpack in the dining room, said a quick hello to my dad and went onto the family room computer to instant message my friends.

    After talking to everyone separately, we all decided to talk in a chartroom so that we could all talk to each other about what we should do. While I was talking to my friends, my mom came home from work and asked me how my day was. I told her what happened and then after talking to her for a few minutes, I decided to go back to the computer and talk to my friends some more.

    All of them were shocked that he shoved me and urged

me to tell someone. I did not want to talk to the principal about it because a part of me felt sorry for Alan. No one at school seemed to like him very much but now I saw why. Later on while I was still on the computer, the phone in the kitchen rang and it was Alan. Before I could even get to the phone to tell him I did not want to talk to him anymore, my mom did it for me. I was relieved I did not have to do it myself because I did not think I would have been able to do it. I did not want to talk to him, but I still felt bad because he had been having a very hard time fitting in.

 I felt just as bad the next day so to cheer me up my parents decided to take Jason and me to the movies. On Monday Allan told me, he was sorry and that it would never happen again and I foolishly believed him. I wish I could tell you that that was the most eventful event in my junior year but it was not.

 In January of that year, after her long battle with cancer my grandmother passed away. I had to go to Pennsylvania to go to her funeral and say goodbye to her. While my family was packing, I went on the computer and I told my friends so they could get my assignments for me. However, I was also going to miss my exams, so I had to talk to my teachers and the school administration so they would know what was going on. Two months went by and I thought my worries were behind me. I was wrong they were just beginning.

 A week after my seventeenth birthday my dad was rushed to the hospital and I found out my dad had stage four-colon cancer. Since I was still in shock about all this, I decided to keep my dad's diagnosis a secret. I also told my mom not to tell the school because I was not ready for them to know yet

One day when I was in my Physics class, my cell phone went off before class started. I was shocked because I had never gotten a call-in class before. Since I didn't want to cause a scene I went out in the hall so I would have some privacy. The call was from my mom and she told me my dad was going to have to stay in the hospital longer than expected.

After speaking to her, I gathered up my belongings and walked out of class. My friends called after me but I did not turn around I kept walking to the main office. Ms. Finnerson was a bitch as usual but I ignored her. When she asked why I was leaving school early, I told her it was none of her business. My mom came, signed me out and we went to the hospital to see my dad. He was doing much worse but he was stable.

A little while later, my brother and his girlfriend Julia showed up to take me home. I told them I wanted to stay with my dad, my mom told me I had to go home so she could take care of my dad. When we got home, I did my homework and Julia made dinner. I did not want to eat but Julia told me to try to eat something. After dinner, I helped Julia make brownies and helped her clean up.

After a while, Jason said he had to run errands and asked us to stay at the house in case my mom called. After a few hours, Julia and I watched TV and I took a shower. After my shower, I let Julia style my hair and went to bed because it was getting late and I had school the next day. The next day at school was a nightmare; my friends kept pestering me all day about why I left class. At lunch, I decided to eat in the library so I could have some peace and quiet. I took out my laptop so I could do some homework, after lunch Julia texted me saying she was on her way to pick me up.

I left the library, went to my locker to get my stuff and then I went to the office where Julia was waiting for me. Unfortunately, Ms. Finnerson was unwillingly to let me go with her since she was not a family member. After hearing, what was going on the principal came out and asked what was going on. I told him I needed Julia to sign me out because my family was at the hospital, and I needed to get there right away. After having me call, my mom to get permission Julia signed me out and we went to the hospital.

After staying there for a few hours, she took me to the mall. She told me I deserved some intense retail therapy. We shopped for a few hours and then she took me home to have dinner. The next day at school was a nightmare. I started to feel sick and I went to the nurse who told me I should go home. She called my house and Jason answered saying that Julia would pick me up and bring me home.

After I grabbed my books and my stuff from my locker, I went to the office to wait for her. When she arrived, Mrs. Finnerson gave her a hard time until I told her to stuff it. Julia smiled at me and we went home. I stayed home from school for the next few days, which was fun because I got a chance to rest and have some peace and quiet.

When I returned to school, I was slightly late because my brother had slept through his alarm. He dropped me off and then I had to go to the office to sign in and get a pass from the secretary. When I arrived, I signed in and then politely asked for a hall pass. Ms. Finnerson laughed and asked me why I was late, did my ride forget about me? That was it; I had had all I was going to take from this nosy lunatic.

"No Mrs. Finnerson my ride didn't forget me this morning. My ride also known as my older brother was busy taking care of my dad and making sure he took his medicine."

I guess I sounded a little snippy because the next thing I knew she said,

"Whoa someone woke up on the wrong side of the bed this morning."

"No I'm just tired of your annoying snarky and smart-ass comments. Now can I please have a pass so I can get to class?"

After a few more laughs she gave me a pass and, I walked out of the office. As I was walking the bell rang for fourth period, I looked at my schedule and went to class. After school, I was heading towards the door so I could catch my bus home when Ms. Finns put a hand on my shoulder to get me to stop and talk to her. I shrugged her off, headed for the door and caught my bus just in time.

When I got home, I did my homework and checked my phone for messages and called my mom to let her know I was home.

When she and my brother got home we had dinner,

and then after a while I went upstairs, got ready for bed, and went to bed. The next day at school, I finally told my friends what was going on. Fortunately, they were really supportive and understanding of my situation. Eventually my dad came home, however he spent most of the summer in and out of the hospital. I tried my best to stay strong and hold down the fort at home so my mother and brother did not have to worry.

 My senior year was even weirder then my junior year. I like to think that my senior year really helped prepare me for the challenges I would face in college however, the year got off to a rocky start. The trouble started the morning before the back to school senior picnic. It started off as any other day at school except that morning I was in a foul mood.

 The day before I found out my dad's cancer spread and the doctor said he only had a year to live. I went to the cafeteria as I always did in the morning and waited for my friends to arrive and the bell to ring. When my friends arrived, I did not say anything I just stared into space and did not really pay attention. My friends asked me what was up but I told them I was not ready to discuss it. I was still feeling melancholic about the news I did not want my dad to die. I was not ready to lose him; he was a major part of my life and I did not know what I do without him. Since I did not want to completely combust and fall apart at school, so I just told myself that maybe the doctors were wrong and he would live longer.

 Later on that day, at lunch, Mille asked me about what

was going on and I told her everything that happened. By the end of the day, I was feeling a little better about things. Eventually it was the end of the day and I had to go home and get ready for the senior class back to school picnic. I did not really want to go but my parents convinced me it would be fun.

When the picnic started, I was having a great time hanging out with friends and relaxing until Allen showed, up and refused to leave me alone. I asked him three times to leave me alone I even walked away, but he would not take a hint. I decided to head to the girl's room to get away from him. I was still nice to him because I was trying to be the bigger person and I felt sorry for him. However even though I felt sorry for him I was still being very cautious.

Eventually I realized that I could not stay in the bathroom all night, so I walked out of the bathroom, and headed back outside to the courtyard. I grabbed a cup of lemonade and then sat down with my friends.

"Gracie where have you been you almost missed the whole party.
"Sorry guys I was trying to avoid Allen he is such a pain.
"He keeps following me around and it's driving me nuts."
"Argh seriously that guy is such a creep"
"When is he going to get the hint that you don't like him?"
"I know but I feel kind of sorry for him, I did get him suspended after all."
"Gracie he shoved you into a pay phone, he deserved what he got."
"Hey, Gracie, I've been looking all over for you."

"Hi Allen, Gracie is busy hanging out with us, why don't you go get some lemonade?"

"I just want to apologize to Gracie, I heard about her father being sick, and I just wanted her to know that if she needs someone to talk to I will be there for her."

"I appreciate that Allen but I don't really like talking about it right now, I just want to enjoy the party and have fun."

"I see well then let's have fun come on let's go get some more lemonade, and then I want to show you something."

"Um ok let's go."

We went to get lemonade and then he grabbed my arm and led me to the library. At one of the tables was a box and he told me to open it. Inside the box was a book on how to deal with a loved one who has cancer. I thanked him for the book and then I started to walk out of the library. I told him I had to meet my friends because they were probably waiting for me.

"Oh come on Gracie, let's just hang out with each other, we don't need those other girls."

"Maybe you don't Allan but they are my best friends and I think I should go back outside and join the party."

I started to walk out of the library and rejoin the party when he put his hand on my shoulder. I told him to let me go and asked him to get his hand off my shoulder.

After getting the message that, I did not want to be bothered he left me alone. After I left the library, I decided to look for my friends and found them sitting at a picnic table. I went over to join them and showed them the book that Alan gave me.

Just then, Alan showed up and tapped me on the shoulder. He asked me if I would like to go with him to get ice cream after the party. I told him no thanks because my friends and I were going to have a sleepover at my house. He was disappointed, but what could I do, I had already promised my friends that we would have our sleepover and it would be rude to cancel at the last minute. He walked away and I foolishly went after him and apologized but he was not having it. He smacked me across the face and punched me in the eye. I walked away and ran into a bathroom. I starting thinking, what should I do about this?

How am I going to face everyone? I cannot go home like this. I decided I would hide in the bathroom until I figured everything out. Eventually the party was over and I realized I had to go out and face the music. When I walked out to the parking lot, my mother was waiting with my friends and she did not look happy. It turned out that one of my classmates had seen Alan hit me and called the police. When the police arrived, Allen was arrested and sent to jail for the night.

Even though Allan went to jail that night, I knew it was not over. After I gave one of the police officers my statement, my mom took us all home and we had our sleepover. I had no desire to talk about what had happened, and luckily, my friends respected that. We just hung out watched movies and ate junk food. The next morning, I awoke to the scent of my mom making blueberry muffins for breakfast. I smiled because those are my favorite kind.

They were also my dad's favorite when I went into the

living room to tell him about the muffins, the room was empty. My friends and I looked all over the house for my dad but could not find him anywhere. I asked my mom where my dad was and she told me he left to go to the hobby shop to buy some parts for his train models.

After breakfast, my mother drove my friends and me to the mall. While we were at the mall, my friends and I bought cool stuff. After two or three hours of shopping and laughing, we decided to stop for the day and my mom picked us up and drove us home. On Monday, everyone was talking about what happened at the back to school BBQ.

Everywhere I went people would stare at me, at times it was hard to deal with but I did the best I could. I just smiled and kept my head held high which helped me feel more confident.

As for psychotic Alan, he received probation, had to stay away from me at all times and a two-week suspension from school. Hearing about his punishment made me feel a little relieved but I tried not to dwell on it. After all, it was my senior year and I had important things to focus on. After many years of perpetration, it was time to fill out college applications. After visiting several schools throughout my high school career, I narrowed it down to Water Crest College and two other schools.

Unfortunately, I forget the names of my backup schools but I decided to apply to Water Crest College first. Water Crest College was my dream school. My father had gone there, and I had seen the campus and fell in love with it. After a few visits to the school, I felt that I fit right in and would be very safe and content there. It would also challenge me because since it was far away I would have to live there, which was going to be a huge change but I knew I could handle it.

When it came time to ask a teacher to write me a letter of recommendation, I picked Mrs. Jones because she had known me since my first year of high school and knew what I was capable of doing and she agreed to write the letter. When it came time to have my guidance counselor Mrs. Chatterworth write one she refused so I had to get my dad to call her and convince her to write one. She did not want to write one because she did not think I was capable of attending Water Crest College.

She told me it was a four-year school and it was going to be too tough for me. The expectations were going to be higher and she did not think an autistic person would be able to handle the demands of a four-year out of state school. After a loud confrontation over the phone with my dad, she wrote the letter. When she asked me to come to her office, I went in, she gave me the letter, and I thanked her. As I got up to leave her office, she told me she did not really have faith that I would get in. I told her I did not care one iota what she thought I knew I was going to get in.

Well I am joyful to report she was wrong about me not getting into Water Crest College. A week before Christmas I was home on school break having an awesome time at home, I got the letter I was waiting for. I was so nervous I started shaking. My mother handed me the letter and I told her I did not want it, because I thought it was a no since it came in a small envelope. My dad told me to read it anyway, so I did I took a deep breath and slowly opened the small envelope.

When I found out, I got into my dream school I was overjoyed. I was also a little proud because I had gotten in to my first-choice college even though some people told me I wouldn't. However, no one was as happy about my acceptance letter as my dad was. He was an alum of Water Crest College; so naturally, it made him proud to have one of his kids at his school.

I was so overjoyed and proud but I knew that getting in was just the beginning. I was going to be in for a bumpy and crazy ride. I was not sure how I was going to tell my friends or my teachers but I hoped when I did they would be happy for me. When school started back up the first thing I did when I saw my friends was show everyone my acceptance letter. All my friends were happy for me, I also told my class advisor Mr. Buffalo and he was happy for me too.

I could not wait to tell my teachers and I thought they would be happy for me. However, when I told the teachers I had in my classes only my math teacher, aquatics teacher and my IEP resource teachers were happy for me. The rest of my teachers and guidance counselor spent a lot of time and effort, trying to persuade me to "do the right thing" and stay home with my sick father.

I knew that was not the real reason they did not want me to go. The real reason was that they thought a four-year school would be too difficult for me. Since I was feeling uncertain if I could really handle leaving home and moving on to the next stage of my life, I went home and I talked to my dad. I told him if he wanted me to stay with him, I would understand. He smiled at me pulled me into his arms and said

"Gracie I do not want you to stay I will be just fine."

"I will miss you but I have your mom, your brother and a team of doctors and nurses, to help me and take care of me. I want you to go to school and get your education."

"Dad what if I can't do it?"

"Honey I know you are scared but I know you will do just fine at Water Crest College."

"You have worked hard for this and I am not going to let you give up your dream."

"I am going to have some rough times ahead but I will be fine and so will you."

"I need you to be my big brave girl right now, I am counting on you and I know you will do your very best."

    I wanted to be my dad's big brave girl but it wasn't going to be easy. I also wanted to believe him but I still was not sure that I could just leave and live on my own for months at a time.

    However, I did not want him to know that so I just smiled at him and told him that as long as my family was okay with it, I was going to go to Water Crest. The next day at school, I told my teachers I was going to Water Crest whether they liked it or not. My teachers however did not stop trying to convince me that I should stay. I found that to be pathetic, because I knew I could do just about anything if I really wanted to.

I knew it was going to be hard but I just hoped that I would find the strength to deal with whatever came my way. However, the troubles were not over yet there were some choppy waters ahead. Three weeks before my 18th birthday, my dad had to go to the hospital due to having a high fever. I received the call in Modern World History, since I did not want to cause a scene; I took a deep breath and tried to stay calm. I stood up, walked out of class and headed to my locker to get my belongings.

As I walked through the halls, I tried not to become emotional but tears started to spill out of my face. After wiping away, the tears, I went to the office and waited for my brother to come pick me up. Since I did not want to speak to Ms. Finnerson, I pulled out a book and started to read. When he arrived he told me to go to the car, and he would be right there. I obeyed and waited for him in the car. Ms. Finnerson gave my brother a hard time about picking me up because he was not my parent or guardian.

My brother told me what that old annoying hag said to him and when I heard what she said I felt; even angrier at her then I did the day before.

"Why didn't your mother come get your sister, is she so lazy that she has to send her son to do things she doesn't want to do?" My brother told me he replied with

"Our mother is with our father who is sick in the hospital; he had an extremely high fever this morning and threw up twice."

"He has been asking for my sister for the past hour and a

half and our mom couldn't leave our dad so I came to get my sister."

According to Jason after Ms. Finnerson heard what was going on she changed her tone. She told him she was sorry about our dad and sincerely hoped that he made a speedy recovery.

My brother walked out of the office and got in the car. We drove in silence to the hospital. When we got to the hospital, my brother and I went straight to the cancer ward. My dad was awake and talking to my mother.

When my brother and I walked in, we both gave him a hug and sat in the chairs. I spent the rest of the day there, until my mom sent us home so we could go have some supper. I told my brother I was not hungry, but he made me eat anyway. We had breakfast for supper and after dinner; I did my homework, took a shower and went to bed.

The next day at school was unbearable. The morning went ok but the afternoon was awful. I had Mr. Gibson for my lunch period class, which meant that after lunch I had to spend three lunch periods with him. I told myself I would keep my temper under control no matter what he said or how many times he pushed my buttons.

I was late to his class because the school counselor asked to speak to me in his office. I liked the school counselor Mr. Winston he was nice and I had worked with him most of my life so I felt comfortable talking to him. He asked me how I was doing since my dad was in the hospital again I told him I was scared. I did not want to lose my dad he was my rock. He told me to stay strong and that he hoped my dad made a fast recovery. After the B and C, lunch bells rang to signal they were over I went to class. I told myself remember keep your temper at bay do not do anything you will regret later.

Unfortunately, all of that went out the window when I walked into the classroom. They were doing ball review to prepare for our test, which was going to happen the following week. As usual, I got my question right, which greatly annoyed Mr. Gibson because he thought I was stupid. Eventually it was time to copy some notes down from the board. When I took my computer out, he threw the ball at it and it just missed my computer by an inch.

I picked my laptop up just in time. I was so wrathful I felt my face getting hotter and hotter with every passing second. I told myself to calm down but it did not work. The ball landed next to my desk, so I put my laptop down, picked up the ball and threw the ball back to him as hard as I could. After I threw the ball at him I started taking a deep breath but suddenly out of nowhere, I started having trouble breathing and started choking. I knew what was happening I was having a panic attack. I started to shake so I went out of the room and to the nurse's office for the remainder of the period. I knew why I had a panic attack it was because I was worried about my dad. If that had not been, bad enough my teacher almost broke my computer.

The nurse asked me what caused me to have a panic attack, and I told her about my dad but not about my teacher nearly breaking my expensive laptop. After I finished talking she gave me some water, after I had had my water, I started to feel a little calmer. She said I was clear to go to my next class. However, I did not go to my next class I went straight to the guidance office to ask if I could speak to my guidance counselor.

When she told me to come in, I told her that I could not stand being in Modern World history. She told me even though she was sorry I was not enjoying the class, I had to stay in it. Feeling frustrated I left her office, but I did not go to class I was too frustrated and upset. I felt that no was on my side or understood the problem. Instead of getting angry or crying, I decided to walk to the library. I sat at a table, put my head in my heads, and tried my best to calm down.

I took some deep breaths and tried to clear my mind. I was so angry and upset I did not know what I was going to do but I knew I had to do something. I could not just sit there acting as if I was a victim. I decided I was going to have to take a stand. I was tired of having to deal with constant bullying every other day by a teacher, who was supposed to be teaching me not bullying and intimidating me. Since I was still feeling angry and did not know what to do or where to go, I just continued to sit at the table.

When the final bell rang, I headed out the door, and went home. When my brother picked me up, he asked me why I looked so angry. I told him what happened from start to finish and he told me that I had to tell mom but should not tell dad. I agreed with my brother, my mom would handle this whole thing a lot better than my dad would. When we got home though I decided not to tell my mom about what happened at school, because I thought she had enough on her plate.

When my mom came home from work, she made dinner and then told me and my brother she was tired so she went to take a nap. I know I probably should have told her but I just could not bring myself to tell her. I figured she had enough to worry about without me adding my issues to her plate. The next day things went by quickly and I had a much better day, even though I did get in trouble for skipping class. Since it was the first time, I only got a warning and two days of lunch detention.

Even though that day was calm, the following day was eventful. I had Mr. Gibson for first period so before the bell rang, I went to my locker to put my computer in my locker. Mr. Gibson saw me and asked me why I was putting my computer in my locker. I slammed my locker door shut and said in an angry voice,
"You know perfectly well why I am putting it in my locker."
"You are the one who chucked the ball at me which almost caused my laptop to fall and break."

He told me he did not mean to it was an accident and I asked him to leave me alone. I also, let him know I was trying to get out of his class, and then he started yelling at me. I do not know why but I started crying and ran off. I did not care where I went I just ran and ran. I ended up running until I ran into the guidance office door and hit my head.

I fell backwards but I got up. Once I was back on my feet, I walked out the door I did not care what my punishment was going to be I was not going to that jerk's class. I started to run and I ran all the way to the convenience store across the street from the high school. I bought myself a lemonade, walked out of the store and sat on the curb. I did not know what to do or who to turn to. Since I did not want to stand there like an idiot, I decided the best thing for me to do was to find a place to go.

One of my choices was, once I finished drinking my lemonade I could find a place to go. Once I found a place to go then I could call my mom, or my brother to come get me and tell them the truth about what was going on. My other choice was I could go back to school and face the music. I chose to be brave and face the music; I walked back into the school with my head held high and went to deal with this mess. I missed Modern World History because I was in the principal's office. I was trying to explain to him, why I ran out of school, and what made me despise Mr. Gibson so much. I told him I needed to get out of Mr. Gibson's class because he made my life a living hell. I told him everything that Mr. Gibson had done.

Once I was finished, the principal told me he understood however, since it was so late in the year, I had to stick it out. It was not what I wanted to hear but I had to accept it. When the bell rang, I went to advisory and then after that I went to the totally waste of time class Literacy. I was somewhat nervous because I did not know how Mrs. Winston was going to react when she saw me. I sat down at my desk and waited for class to start.

When class started, she acted as if everything was normal so I decided to do the same. Once class is over however she asked me to stay behind so we could talk. She started with she was shocked that I had skipped her class the other day. After all it was me she was talking to, I never skipped a class or did anything bad ever. I told her I had a meltdown and it would not happen again.

After a few seconds of awkward silence, I started to walk out of the room. She asked me where I was going. I responded with to class. I walked away because I did not want to be late and ran into Mr. Gibson. As I was walking off to class, I saw him but I did not look or speak to him. He called my name but I kept walking. Tears were stinging my eyes and I did not know why but I knew what I needed to do. I needed to go to gym class. Unfortunately when I arrived to class I was late but only by a few minutes.

I hurried and changed into my gym clothes and headed out to join my friends. Millie handed me a racket and we started playing bag mitten. We continued to play until it was time to go to lunch and then after lunch I headed to ceramics. I loved ceramics because I could just sit there and work on my project without anyone bothering me.

When class started, we all grabbed our projects and got to work. I was working on a ceramic title box, which was going to be a birthday gift for my aunt. After class was over I went to math and then I went home for the day.

A week before my birthday my dad came home and he asked me what I wanted to do for my birthday. After all he said an eighteenth birthday is special. I told him that I was going to have the family party the day before and on my birthday; I was going to go out with my friends. He seemed to be ok with that so that is what we did.

The day before my birthday, I had a small quiet family party with my mom, dad and brother. It was nice and the presents were nice too. I got a pink and white camcorder, new clothes, a new cellphone and ice blue heels to match my prom dress. I was so excited about my gifts I started filming everyone with my new camcorder. Even though I enjoyed filming, everyone my family was getting pretty annoyed with me so I stopped recording.

The next morning, I went downstairs to find blueberry muffins, bacon and fruit waiting for me. My mom smiled, and everyone wished me a happy birthday. After breakfast, my mom took me to school. At school, I had a party and when the school day was over, I waited for my mom to pick me up. When she arrived, I got in the car and we headed to my friends' houses and picked everyone up. My mom dropped us off at the ice cream shop, after we had our ice cream we got a ride to the mall and went shopping. I felt like the luckiest girl in the world. After shopping my friends surprised me and took me out to dinner, and had the waiter sing happy birthday. When I got home, I watched a home movie with my dad and eventually went to sleep.

When it came time for prom, I was very excited. My friends decided we were getting a limo and we were going as a group since none of us had dates. When the big night finally arrived, I went to the hair salon and got my hair and nails done. After that, I went home to put on my dress, shoes and makeup. When I walked down the stairs, my dad started taking pictures. As my dad was taking pictures, I felt like a movie star getting ready for a night at an award show.

When my friends arrived, we took pictures and then it was off to prom. When we arrived at the ballroom, where the prom was located, it was as beautiful as I could have imagined. After a while, Angelo surprised me by asking me to dance. We stayed on the dance floor for what seemed like forever and I felt like the most important girl in the world. As we danced I felt as beautiful and specials as a princess at an elegant ball. We danced until my friends tapped me on the shoulder and told me dinner was being served. As I started to walk towards the table, I felt like this was all a dream and at any moment I was going to wake up.

  The food was great but I was not hungry. I wanted to go back on the dance floor and dance some more. I was having a great time at the dance until our class advisors announced that it was time to find out who was going to be crowned prom king and queen of the dance. To everyone's surprise, Angelo was prom king and I was prom queen. I was so stunned I could barely speak. I did not realize that I was so popular.

  Everything was wonderful until it came time for me to receive my crown. As I walked over towards the DJ both to receive my crown, Allan and Amy started throwing water balloons at me and I got soaking wet. My dress was drenched and so was my hair I looked and felt awful. I was so wrathful and hurt I did not know what to say I honestly just wanted to sink into the floor and disappear.

  After a few awkward moments of silence, Allan and Amy cleaned up their mess and the dance continued as if nothing happened. Mary the class president placed the crowns on our heads, Angelo took my hand, and we had our dance. After the king and queen dance, I left the ballroom called my mom and asked her to come get me.

When she arrived and asked me what happened to my dress, I burst into tears and told her what my so-called friends had done. Once I had finished telling her what happened, she asked me if I wanted her to call the school to complain. I told her I would handle it on my own I also asked her not to tell my dad because I did not want to upset him.

When I got home, my mom told me my dad was probably upstairs sleeping. I went into my room changed into my pajamas and got ready for bed. After that, my phone started ringing, but I just let it go to voicemail because I was not in the mood to talk to anyone. I just went to bed and hoped that everyone would have forgotten about what happened. I was glad the prom was over and even though I did not want to, I sobbed, like a baby until I fell asleep. I don't even know why I was crying but I just let myself cry because I knew once I was done crying I would feel better.

At school on Monday, Amy and Alan tried to act as if nothing had happened which really made my blood boil. When they tried to speak to me, I walked away and told them to leave me alone. For the rest of the year I hung out with Millie and my other friends.

As time went by a part of me was melancholic to leave but I was also excited for the journey ahead of me. A week before the graduation ceremony, my teachers who were against me going to Water Crest College cornered me during my resource class. They sat me down and asked me if I was sure, I was doing the right thing.

    I took a deep breath and then I told them I had made my choice, and there was no turning back. At the end of the summer in August, I was moving to New Hampshire. They told me I was selfish because I was going to be leaving my cancer-stricken dad behind. When I heard that, it was like a slap in the face. I was so livid I told them that I would give anything to have my dad come with me but it was impossible. I was so livid I could feel my face getting warmer and warmer. Since I did not want to get in trouble, I took a deep breath and tried to calm down.

    After I was calmer, I told them going to Water Crest College was something I was going to have to do on my own, with or without their support, and then I walked away. I was done with insignificant teachers who did not know anything about my situation or about how hard it was. I started getting upset again so I decided to run I ran all the way to the guidance office, hit my head on the door, and passed out.

    When I woke up I was in the nurse's office and she was asking me if I could hear her. I sat up and discovered that there was a large bump on my head, which she was treating with an ice pack. After a few minutes, she told me she was going to call my parents to come get me and take me home. However, since my dad was having chemo and my mom was with him, my brother came to get me, and took me to the doctor.

    The doctor examined the bump and told me I was fine

so I went home. My brother was asking me a bunch of questions but I was not giving him any answers. I was still too angry and confused to talk about it. When we arrived back home, I told Jason I had a rotten day at school and I was going to my room to lie down. Fortunately, Jason gave me some space and I was able to digest everything that had happened.

The next day at school my teachers asked to talk to me, but I shook my head I was through talking to them about this. I was going to have to figure this out on my own. I walked right past them and went to class. Throughout the day, I was thinking about what I should do about the whole college thing but I could not really come up with a conclusion. Since I was feeling really frustrated and confused I decided to talk to Mr. Winston about it again, after all he was always able to give me great advice so I thought it couldn't hurt to talk to him.

After listening to me talk for a while, he asked me what I really wanted. After taking a deep breath, I told him what I wanted more than anything in the world was to go to Water Crest College. He laughed and told me I had solved my own problem. He told me it was not important what my teachers thought, or my parents or even my brother. I was the only one who could make this decision and that was what being an adult was all about.

After I spoke with Mr. Winston, I felt better and knew what my choice was going to be. I decided I was going to go to Water Crest College whether those meddlesome busybodies supported me or not. When I saw them in the hall, I marched up to them and told them in a polite but firm voice, that I respected their opinions but I had made my choice. I told them I spent a long time thinking about it and decided I was going to Water Crest College. When they tried to interrupt, I told them I was not finished. I added that I did not need them to approve or agree with my choice, but I did need them to respect my choice.

After a few minutes, they tried to tell me I was making a mistake but I just turned around and walked away. I realized I was just wasting my breath; they were never going to support me. When it came time to take my exams I did my very best and passed every single one, including my math exam. When I received my grades on my exams, I felt pleasantly surprised and proud. I had never done that well on exams before but I guess all that hard work and studying I had done had paid off.

After exams, Mr. Gibson came up to me, and once again told me what a horrible person I was. I told him to get a life and walked away. I was so content and relieved that I was graduating, that I did not care what he or any of the other imbecile teachers thought anymore. Their opinions meant nothing to me and I decided I was going to enjoy the rest of my senior year and avoid any more drama.

When the graduation ceremony finally came around, I was excited but also nervous. When it was time to start getting lined up for the ceremony, I made sure my graduation cap was securely on my head and my graduation robe was neat and clean. After a few minutes of taking pictures with classmates, it was time to walk down the aisle and sit in our assigned seats. As I walked down the aisle, I thought about the life I was leaving behind and the life that I was about to start.

Once I sat down, I took a deep breath and waited for my turn to walk across the stage. When it was finally my turn, I graciously walked up the steps shook my principal's hand and grabbed my diploma. After my diploma was in my hand, I walked down the stairs and walked graciously back to my seat. After all the graduates had their diplomas, we threw our caps into the air and walked out to change our clothes for the post-graduation party.

As I changed my clothes, I became more and more excited to attend the party. I quickly changed my clothes, took pictures with my friends, my favorite teachers and my family. After all the pictures and well wishes, I said goodbye to everyone, and headed onto one of the buses that were parked outside waiting to take all of us graduates to the party. After everyone was on the buses, we headed to the post-graduation party.

After the long bus ride, all of the graduates went into a building. Inside the building we walked down a flight of stairs and into a room with a table of food and drinks set up on it. There were also a bunch of other tables with plates, napkins and silverware were set up as well. I sat with Millie and some of my other friends and we all wound up having a fantastic time. Even though I was having a great time with my friends, I was tired and eventually fell asleep on a couch.

When I woke up, it was time to cut the cake. After we all stuffed our faces with cake we played games, laughed and danced until it was time to go. As the buses pulled away, I started to think about my future. I thought about what college was going to be like and the friends I was going to make there. I also was worried about what was going to happen to my father after I left. He told me he would be safe and I wanted to believe him, but I did not.

When we arrived back at the school, I got into my parents car without speaking a word to anyone. I did not want to spoil everyone else's good time by being a downer so I told my parents I just wanted to go home. Later on that day, my parents took my brother and I out for dinner, there was a congratulatory toast given, and they gave me presents. I felt so loved and special, and I wished that it would always be like this but life does not always grant us our wishes. If you keep reading, you will understand why I said this.

The Summer before College and the College Years

Dear Diary,

    The summer before college was just like all the other summers of my life. I spent my time with my family and hung out with friends. I did not want to think about leaving for college until I had to. I knew I was going to have to face it eventually, but I just wanted to enjoy my last summer before college with my family and friends. My dad's health was up and down but I tried my best to stay positive for both his sake and my own.

    The person I spent the most time with was my dad, I really loved that time I spent with him just the two of us. We spent almost every day at a small hobby shop a few towns away, so my dad could purchase the supplies he needed for his model of a train station. He was making it himself and it was taking a long time but it kept him busy, ad helped him relax after going through all his various cancer treatments.

    After choosing the trains and parts my dad wanted, we would check out, leave the hobby shop, and head home or if my dad was feeling up to it we would go get something to eat. I loved spending time with my dad, and I was really going to miss him but I decided to just smile and make the most of the time we had together.

    One day as we were having lunch at a Mexican

restaurant, my dad kept laughing and telling me he couldn't believe his little girl was all grown up and going off to college. He said it seemed like just yesterday I was going off to kindergarten and wearing that adorable white and red - checkered dress with the shiny black buckle shoes. As he talked, I rolled my eyes. I could not believe my dad was getting nostalgic over the fact that I was all grown up and leaving home.

I told him that I was still his little girl, and even though I was moving to New Hampshire, I would come home occasionally to visit and see how he was doing. I did not want to let on that I was really going to miss him because I did not want to fall apart in front of him. I decided I was going to be strong for both of us and make sure that I did everything I could to make this summer the best summer ever.

Over the next few weeks of the summer, I hung out with family and friends. I had a small graduation party and then that was that. Nothing else mattered to me. I was moving on and moving forward with my future. I was not sure what was ahead of me but I knew whatever it was I was going to make the best of it and stay focused on my goals.

As the final weeks of summer went on I tried not to be sad about leaving but it was hard because I was going to a completely new place where I did not know anyone. After a few minutes I realized that maybe, it was a good thing that I was going somewhere new because when I arrived at school I could have a fresh start. I started to pack up my belongings and imagine what my new life in New Hampshire would be like.

It was a crazy day when I left home and moved from my comfortable life in RI to a new life in Water Lilianna New Hampshire. Over the summer, I had been trying to imagine what my college life would be like. I wondered about the kind of people I would meet and what my professors and classes would be like. I was also hoping I was going to be safe in the dorm I was going to be living in. However, nothing I imagined could have even held a candle to what happened.

My first day went smoothly, and I could tell I was going to love it there. People seemed nice and friendly. However, I could not help feeling somewhat shy and out of place. I had never felt more far away from home before in my life. As the day went on, I felt more and more homesick because every other time I had traveled I was with a family member or friends. I had never been without people I knew around me before. I got along ok with my roommate, but she and I were completely different.

Eventually she moved out, and to be honest I was somewhat happy when she did. After she moved out, I got closer to the other girls in my hall. They were really nice and friendly; I also had made some friends that did not live in my hall.

However, despite all the friends and nice people I was still homesick and worried about my dad almost all the time. At first, I did not tell anyone about my dad but after a leak from the radiator in my room caused a flood, I told my area coordinator what was going on. After I told her, what was going on she asked one of the counselors from the health center to help support and look out for me.

I loved going to the health center many of the counselors and staff there were kind and seemed to genuinely care and support the students. It became a safe space for me to go and talk about whatever was on my mind. Another thing that helped support me was I found a special place that I could go when I was feeling homesick or just plain sad. I was walking around exploring when I came across the covered bridge.

It was old-fashioned looking and it smelled like old wood and soot. Since I was feeling somewhat curious, I decided to walk across and see where it would take me. I walked and then I came across the gravel path and I continued walking.

As I was walking, I realized I had been there before. I remembered my father had taken my brother and me there once when we visited the college when I was younger. I laughed and saw all the trees and plants the leaves had not changed yet. They were still the beautiful leafy green color but it was only the beginning of September. I assumed the leaves would not change until early October.

I continued to walk and saw a nice spot to stop and rest so I did. I went down the little hill and sat on the rock. I looked around it was peaceful and quiet and I liked that I felt safe there. I started tossing brown acorns into the water and decided to put my feet in the water. The water felt cold but I did not care I was having fun.

I was no longer worrying about my dad I was at peace.

I looked around at the trees the river and even the small dirt mound that looked like a random island and felt so peaceful and happy, I decided to hang out there for a while. I also decided that this was going to be the place I would go when I was sad or scared. I went there a lot sometimes I brought friends and other times I went alone. I needed to go there because there, I could cry, or scream without anyone overhearing me. The river was a comfort and I felt safe there, I felt like I was invincible there nothing could touch me or hurt me while I was there.

One day I was hanging out with two friends there, and I fell in the water. Fortunately, my friends pulled me out. We all started laughing and then they walked me back to my room so I could change my clothes. It was a great place to go to get things off my mind; it was safe and gave me a chance to get away from people if I needed to. However, I would need more than the river and counseling to get through what happened next.

A few short months after I had first discovered my special place my life was about to change forever. It was just an ordinary school day for me. The sun was shining in the sky. It was a beautiful and crisp fall afternoon in New Hampshire and I had just had lunch with my friends Sandy, Susan and Carol.

I was gathering my books for Food and World History when my cell phone went off. It was my mom and it was the call I had been dreading. My dad was dying and did not have much more time to live and I needed to get home as soon as possible. I packed my bag and texted my friends saying that I had to go home for a while and that I would be returning on Sunday. Sandy knew something was wrong so she and Carol ran to my room.

When they got there, they opened my unlocked door, and found me on my bed with my face buried in my pillow. I was crying and they did not even have to ask me why. All they said was

"It's your dad isn't it?" I said yeah I told them he was dying and did not have much time left to live. We talked and waited for my mom's friend to come get me and bring me to the hospital to see my dad. When she arrived, my friends walked outside with me to The Lounge.

We hugged and I told them to look out for each other while I was gone. I also told them not to worry about me I was going to be fine. Of course, I was lying through my teeth but I was doing it because I did not want them to worry.

When Candice and I got in the car, she told me that she had tissues in case I needed to cry. Even though I felt like crying, I could not cry while in the car. I wanted to but no tears came I do not know why I had cried a lot about this very moment and yet suddenly I had no tears left.

I guess I was just trying to be strong and show no fear or weakness. To keep myself from crying and losing strength I focused on the trees that we kept passing. Unfortunately, that strength left me as soon as Candice and I walked into the hospital room and I saw my dad. He looked weak and helpless so I went over to give him a hug. He looked at me and smiled. I stayed in the room for a little while but after the doctor came in, I lost it. I excused myself and walked out of the room sat in a chair and cried my eyes out. As I, sat there crying like a baby a nurse offered me a box of tissues. I thanked her and blew my nose.

I picked up my phone and called Millie my best friend in the world. She was shocked when I told her because the last time we had spoken my dad was ok. I stayed out there until all the tears were gone because I knew if my dad saw me crying he might start crying too. After that, my mom took me to the cafeteria to get something to eat. I asked her how much longer dad had and she said she did not know. She also told me there was not anything else the doctors could do for him.

After we ate, I left the hospital my brother took me home and then went out with his friends because it was his birthday. He did not want to go out but I told him that he should. I told him after all it was his birthday and he should enjoy it. I sat at home watched home movies and then although I do not remember doing this I went upstairs to bed.

Around two in the morning, my mom woke me up to tell me my dad was gone. I cried and then went downstairs to watch TV and to post on social media that my dad had passed on. I also text messaged my friends and let them know what happened. Eventually I went back upstairs to bed it was hard to go back to sleep, but eventually I fell asleep.

When I woke up the scent of blueberry muffins was filling the air. For a split second, I thought that that I had been dreaming, but I had not it was true my dad was gone.

Blueberry muffins were my dad's favorite so I think my mom was just trying to make us feel better.

However even though I acted otherwise I felt worse. After I ate my muffins, I went back upstairs to lie down on my bed and I closed and locked the door. I did not feel like talking or dealing with anyone. I was trying to wake up from this nightmare even though I knew it was not a nightmare my dad was gone. That day the phone continued ringing off the hook with people calling to check on us. I could tell although she tried not to show it, my mother was upset that my dad died.

Since I did not want to bother my mother with my own feelings, I went outside to my Japanese maple. I sat in the fort that my brother and I had made all those years ago. I remember showing my dad the fort and he was very impressed. I just sat there and laid down on the dirty mulch. I closed my eyes and I told myself when I opened my eyes I would be back at school and my father would be fine. I opened my eyes it did not work I was at home and my father was dead. I stayed at the tree until it got dark and then I brushed myself off and went back inside.

Around suppertime, my friends had called me, when I got off the phone my mother had arrived with Chinese takeout. I ate even though I did not want to and then cleaned up so that my mother would not have a fit. After I cleaned up the doorbell rang and it was our neighbors from across the street we also had a surprise visit from Lexie and her mom. Apparently they had moved back and I was really excited to see her again.

They made the cookies that Lexie and I used to make when we were little at her house during snow days. I could not believe she remembered and I was happy to see her. After saying goodbye to Lexie and her mom and thanking them for the cookies, I decided that I was going back to school the next day. On the way back to school, I tried to be as quiet as possible. My mom tried to make it seem like everything was going to be ok but I think we both knew that things would not be okay for a long time.

When we arrived at school my mother and I got out of the car and started unloading my things. After we unloaded, my mom left, and I took a nap. After my nap, Sandy came over and we went to the Lounge. I did not say much on the walk over but I did not have to, she knew I was mourning. We arrived at the Lounge Center and we spoke to my mentor Jan and then Susan arrived and we went to the health center. We spoke to Irene a counselor at the Wellness center and then went to the cafeteria to get something to eat.

For the next several weeks, I did not really do much except exercise, eat when I felt like it, go to class, do homework, and hang out with friends. I did not eat with them I ate alone but I would go to their rooms to watch movies or play video games. Concerned about my behavior my friends went to talk to my resident assistant Sam about my strange new habits. Everyone was getting concerned about my new habits and behavior. However, every time someone tried to talk to me about it I was either asleep or too busy to talk.

A few more weeks went by and I started cutting myself

and became depressed. At an all-night party hosted by the school, I passed out and I woke up feeling so embarrassed. After a few minutes of just sitting there, I stood up and was lead to another room to talk to my Area Coordinator Kayla and my least favorite campus safety officer Louie."

"Gracie what is going on do you know what caused you to pass out tonight?"

"I wasn't feeling well and I felt dizzy but other than that I am not sure what caused me to pass out."

After a few minutes, Louie snorted.

"I know why Gracie passed out because she is an attention whore and enjoys when all eyes are on her."

"No I don't, I hate when I am the center of attention, oh screw this I'm done have a great night and life I am going to bed."

After telling them how I felt I stood up and left. They called after me but I ignored them and kept walking. Instead of going to bed, I decided to go back to the party. The party was fun but eventually I decided I needed to go back to my room and get some rest.

After the party things took a turn for the worse, I started cutting more and more often. I was able to hide the cutting at first, but then after an emotional breakdown one of the girls on my floor got our resident assistant. When Sam arrived, I was still crying so he patiently waited for me to calm down long enough for me to tell him what was going on.

When I finally told him everything he said he had to talk to his boss Kayla the Area Coordinator about what was happening, he did not have a choice. He told me to wait in my room until he got back and we would figure out what to do from there. Once he had left, I grabbed my stuffed dog Huffy and hid under the bed. I know that seems childish but I was terrified and it was the only place to hide in my room.

Eventually after what seems like forever Sam came back and Kayla, and Louie were with him. They knocked on the door but I was too scared to open it. After a few more knocks, Sam used a key and opened my door.

They looked around the room to see if they could find me. I tried to say as quiet as possible and if I hadn't sneezed, they wouldn't have found me. When they did, I crawled out from under the bed and faced the music. After I came out from underneath the bed, we all went to the duty office to have a private conversation.

I had to agree to a few conditions and a safety contract and then Kayla, Sam and Louie took me back to my room. Once we were back in my room, I grabbed anything sharp that I could cut myself with and put it in the box that Louie had put on my bed. After every sharp object was on my bed, Louie grabbed the box and left my room with Sam and Kayla following behind him.

After Sam, Kayla and Louie left I looked around my room and began cleaning it, and for some reason cleaning made me feel better. After I cleaned every surface in my room, I went to bed. As I lay in bed, I thought about what my dad would have said to me if he knew what was going on with me.

I knew he would probably be very disappointed in me

and maybe even angry, but I think he also would have tried to understand. My father was the type of man that even when you did something wrong he would still love and support you. It did not matter how awful what you had done was he would still care and want what was best for you.

 Since they were concerned about my safety, my counselor called my mom and told her what had been happening at school. To help me feel better I guess, my mom came up to visit me and tried to understand what was going on. Eventually it was time for Christmas break and unlike the rest of the students in my dorm; I was not looking forward to going home. This was going to be the first Christmas that I was going to celebrate without my dad and I knew it was going to be lousy.

 However, like it or not unless I wanted to pay extra money for my room I had to go home and celebrate Christmas with my family. Instead of our usual quiet just us Christmas, that year my mom decided, we were going to go to Allentown Pennsylvania. Normally I was the first one in the car when we would go to Pennsylvania, however this time I really did not want to go. I did not want to see or deal with anyone. However, my mom was not going to let me stay home, therefore, whether I liked it or not I was spending Christmas in Allentown.

 When we finally arrived, we walked into the house, I hugged and kissed my grandfather, my uncle and his girlfriend and saw the beautiful decorations and the ornaments on the Christmas tree. My grandfather had outdone himself but I was not really in the Christmas spirit.

We unpacked the car, spent a little time with my family, and went to bed. When I went to bed I was really missing my dad, but I tried my best not to show it and just closed my eyes.

The next morning there were presents everywhere there were so many presents, I did not know where to start. My grandfather started laughing and told us to start opening the gifts already. After a little while, my Uncle Buddy, his girlfriend Jane, his two kids Freddy and Benny, my aunt's sister Melody and her daughter Lucy showed up. After they arrived more gifts, laughs and holiday cheer filled my grandfather's house.

. It was truly awesome to be with everyone but a part of me felt sad because my dad and my nana were not there to celebrate with us. The gifts were all wonderful and I loved seeing the smiles on everyone's faces when they saw what they got but there was a sadness in the air that I couldn't ignore.

After all the presents were opened and the ripped wrapping paper was cleaned up, we sat around and caught up with each other. Talking and catching up with everyone was nice but I still felt something missing. Unfortunately, I did not have a lot of time to dwell on it because we were going to my Aunt Mary's house to open more gifts.

When we got there, my Aunt Mary had fresh cookies and other food waiting for us. After we all stuffed our faces with cookies and food, we opened presents. After that, we all went to a local restaurant to have our holiday meal. At the restaurant, we had an amazing meal and even more amazing desert. It was nice to be with my family, and for a little while I was able to forget about being sad and missing my dad. Later on that night when I was going to sleep, I could not help but feel lucky and grateful that I had a loving and supportive family.

Eventually we went back home and did stuff together just the three of us, which was also nice. As a great surprise Julia came to visit us, I was so happy to see her again I cried. She just smiled and gave me a big hug and asked me how I was doing. My brother had asked her to come because even though they were not together anymore they were still good friends. Having Julia around was like having the older sister around that I always wanted. She took me shopping; we baked cookies, and watched our favorite television shows together

It was nice being with her and spending time with her helped distract me from the pain of losing my dad. I started to feel like things just might start getting back to normal.

After a few weeks, Julia went back home and I went back to school. It was a new semester and I was determined to make sure that I made it work. The first few weeks were okay but after the first, few weeks' things took a turn for the worst.

My grades were perfect; in fact, I was doing really well academically. However, trouble was brewing; a new friend joined the crew her name was Gloria. At first, she was nice and I thought we could be friends. However, as the weeks went by she showed her true colors and turned my other friends against me.

It started with little things like excluding me from trips, and not hanging out with me as much but the worst was yet to come. After a particularly nasty fight, Gloria convinced them to start spreading lies about me to anyone who was willing to listen. Due to those lies and because no one was willing to listen to my side of the story, I was sent home for a weekend.

I still remember what happened that day. I went to the health center and I heard one of the counselors call my mother a bad mother, I was so wrathful I marched up the stairs and told her off. I will spare you the details of the language I used but let's just say the rainbow isn't as colorful as the curse words that came out of my mouth.

After I finished yelling and telling her off I went back to my dorm room. Fortunately once I got to my room I was able to calm down. I packed a bag and my mother picked me up. Having the weekend off at home helped a little but I was still depressed.

Even though I was depressed and at times I wanted to give up, I made the decision to not allow my depression or my backstabbing ex-friends get to me. Instead of doing that I did everything in my power to enjoy the rest of my freshman year of college. My ex friends would occasionally try to speak to me but I would always just walk away. I did not have anything to say to them because to be honest to me it just did not seem worth it. They were backstabbing little backstabbers and could go kick rocks for all I cared. I didn't care about them anymore because they obviously didn't care about me.

For the rest of the semester I kept my head down and, focused on my work. I was done with people at this school and I was done with the drama. I was so livid I could not even think straight. I felt very isolated and alone because I did not know whom I could trust so I chose not to trust anyone. I could not believe that instead of listening to both sides of the story, the administration and the Res life staff just accepted what my ex friends had to say. I was so livid; that I decided I was no longer going to be friends with those pathetic bitches anymore.

After a month I decided to go home for another weekend. I needed a break from school, and I couldn't handle people looking at me, and whispering about me behind my back. While I was home, I did homework and stayed in my room all weekend. I did not want to see or talk to anyone and fortunately, my mom and brother respected my wishes. My fake friends tried to call me but I ignored their calls. When I returned to campus, I kept my head down and focused on the work that needed to be done.

Two weeks before the final exams, the school put on a party for the students, so that they could celebrate the end of the school year. They also wanted the students to blow off some steam before final exams started, so that we would all feel relaxed and not make poor choices.

Instead of going to the end of year celebration, I ended up watching movies and listening to music in my room and ended up having a great time. I also got some extra studying done too so I would definitely pass my final exams. My RA came to my room and tried to convince me to go and join in the fun but I told him to go away and leave me alone.

The day before exams, my ex friends came over. When they knocked on the door I opened the door but I didn't invite them in. Instead I told them to leave and never contact me again. When they refused to leave, I slammed the door in their faces.

Over the next few days, they kept trying to talk to me but I tried to ignore them. However ignoring them did not work so I told them if they ever contacted me, again I would file a restraining order. They finally got the message and left me alone.

The next day I was studying for an exam when I heard knocking on my door so I walked, over to the door and opened it. It was my R.A Sam and some of his coworkers. They asked if they could come in to speak to me just for a few minutes. I told them there was nothing they could say, and then graciously asked them to leave.

Reluctantly they left closing my door behind them. Once they were gone I grabbed a piece of paper from my desk and wrote studying please do not disturb and taped it to my door. Fortunately, that worked and I was able to study and finish my work without being disturbed.

After my last exam, I packed up my stuff, and I made sure that every inch of my dorm room was in pristine condition. Once I was sure that every inch of the room was pristine, I went to bed.

The next morning my mom came and I was so enthusiastic to see her I cried. After we caught up for a few minutes, we loaded up the car and then she waited in the car while I checked out of my dorm room. I walked over to the duty office and told the R.As that I was ready to checkout. The R.As tried to talk to me but I would not respond. When they asked me why I was acting so cold and distant, I snapped.

"I am not acting cold and distant. I just want to quickly check out of my dorm room so I can leave and get the hell out of here."

"Gracie calm down, we are sorry for what happened to you."

"It's a little late for an apology, don't you think?"

"Gracie…"

"Where the fucking hell was the apology when I was forced to go home for a weekend?"

"Gracie just let us explain our side of the story."

I was so livid at that comment that I gave an involuntary snort in response, took a deep breath and then came out with the perfect comeback.

"After I didn't get to explain my side you expect me to stand here and listen to yours?"

"No offense you guys but that is really hypocritical don't you think?"

"We didn't know that you were going to get sent home for the weekend."

"We thought the administration was going to talk to you and ask that you seek some extra help and support"

"Well that's not what happened is it?"

"Instead of getting extra help and support I got sent home and humiliated. If that wasn't bad enough, my mother was called a bad mother."

"Gracie…"

"I'm fine I honestly don't want to talk about this anymore, all I want is to check out and go home please."

"Okay well you are all set have a nice summer."

"Thank you I will I hope you have a nice summer break too goodbye."

When I finally walked back to my mother's car I apologized to her for taking so long and then explained what happened. When I told her what happened, she was furious but we both decided it was not worth getting all worked up about it and drove home.

When I was finally home, I was joyous but I did not stay home though. A few days after I came home I told my mom I did not want to be in RI. After talking about where I could possibly go my mom's family in England invited me to stay with them. After talking to my relatives my mom decided, I could go to England and stay there for the remainder of the summer.

While I was in England, I saw a therapist and hung out with my aunts, uncles and cousins. I loved being in England because I did not have to think about school and the people who had hurt me there. While I was gone, my friends from home asked my mother where I was but she would not tell them. I had asked her not to because I did not want them to know what had happened. They would email me and call me but I would not respond until one day I finally caved and wrote them a cryptic email. I told them I was going to be gone for the whole summer and I would see them in the fall at thanksgiving. Mille called me and asked me where I was and asked if I was okay.

"Gracie are you alright where are you?"

"Hi, Millie, I'm fine and I can't tell you where I am but I can't tell you, I am alright."

"I'm glad you are alright but why can't you tell me where you are?"

"It's too complicated to explain right now."

"Look Millie I have to go but I will call you later okay?"

"Okay I guess but where are you?"

"I can't tell you but I will tell you everything when I come home."

"Okay bye"

"Bye."

    I felt terrible about not telling Millie more information but I was not ready to talk. Later on that night, my cousin Louisa and I were up late talking and she asked me to tell her about what happened to me at school. I began to tell her but then I started crying and she hugged me and told me I did not have to talk until I was ready. I enjoyed being in England and reuniting with my family.

    Every day I would help my cousin Louisa with her chores and then we would walk around London. Even though I was having fun in London, I still missed everyone back home in America. I talked to Mille and my mom at least once a day and I missed them but I was also glad to be away so I could have a chance to think. One day after checking my email, I found out my former friends from college were looking for me. They asked everyone they could think of but fortunately, no one told them where I was.

After reading the email, I was furious. I could not believe they still had the nerve to attempt to harass and bother my family and friends from home. A part of me wanted to call them and ask them if, they had any shame or guilt about what they did at all, but then I decided it was not worth it. It was for the best if I did not bother with them and just focused on enjoying my vacation reconnecting with family.

. The next day I spent the day shopping and visiting various places in England with Louisa. I could not believe all the majestic places there were to go to in England and a part of me was feeling a little overwhelmed but I decided to just relax and go with the flow. When we would stop somewhere, we would take turns taking pictures and try to get a souvenir from each place we stopped at.

As we walked around I saw parents walking around with kids I started to feel slightly homesick but I was still glad I came. Coming to England and getting away from everything was the right thing to do. I was having a blast and for the first time in a long time, I was starting to eel content and safe again and to me that was the best part of all.

One day my Aunt Marie and Uncle William decided to take us on a surprise trip. After bugging them for a few days, they finally told us where we would be going. We were going to spend a few weeks in France and Italy.

A few weeks went by and then it was time to go on our trip. My relatives took us everywhere and we took a ton of pictures in all the places we visited. Eventually after spending the last week of the trip in Paris, we went back to

England.

I really loved Paris we had an amazing time there taking in all of the sights was amazing and the food was incredible. Both the countries we visited were breathtaking and I could not wait to call my mom to tell her all about it. When we got back to England, I called my mom to tell her all about the trip and that we had gotten back safely. I was having so much fun I wanted to stay in England forever. I loved being with my family and seeing new sights and eating different foods. Every day was an adventure, and I was always excited and joyful to see what the day would bring.

Unfortunately, eventually my time in England ended and I flew back home to RI. Before I left Louisa and I exchanged email addresses so we could keep in touch with each other. It was hard to say goodbye I had had an amazing time and could not wait to tell my mom and brother all about it. After saying my goodbyes, I thanked my England family for letting me visit and then Louisa drove me to the airport. In the car, we talked about maybe having her and some other family members coming to visit me at some point.

At the airport Louisa walked me all the way to security and then we hugged goodbye and On the plane, I thought about my trip and how much fun I had visiting my family.. I was sad to leave but I knew I had to go home and spend time with my family from home. I was not sure what to expect after being gone for most of the summer but when I got off the plane, I received a warm welcome back home. While in the car my mother and my brother kept asking me different questions about my trip, and I did my best to answer them.

When I arrived home, I unpacked my clothes and tried to adjust to being back home after being away for so long. Later that night my mom made me my favorite dinner, chicken, mash potatoes and corn on the cob. After dinner, we had a quiet celebration to welcome me home.

For the last week of my summer vacation, I hung with my mom and my brother. I also visited with Millie and that was slightly awkward.

"Gracie welcome home I've missed you."

"I missed you too Millie, how has the summer been treating you?"

"Pretty good, okay enough small talk where have you been for the past few months?"

"Wow okay well I've been traveling and putting my life back together."

"Where did you go?"

"I've been in England, France and Italy."

"Let me get this straight while I've been here in RI, you've been in Europe and the United Kingdom?"

"Yes I stayed with relatives, I am sorry if I upset you but after having a very turbulent year at school I needed to go somewhere else for a few weeks."

"Why didn't you just tell me what was going on?" I'm your best friend I would have been there for you."

"I wanted to tell you but I was embarrassed I'm sorry."

"Well you shouldn't have been in case you have forgotten I have been by your side through a ton of embarrassing moments.

"I know I'm sorry I just needed some time and being in other countries really helped me, I didn't have to think about how hurt or broken I felt."

"Do you still feel hurt and broken?"

"No but I really am sorry I didn't tell you what was going on. School was vile this year, my so-called college friends turned on me, and I almost got sent home."

"Okay I forgive you but please no more secrets."

"I promise no more secrets."

Eventually it was time for me to go back to school and face the music. I was nervous and excited to be going back and start the new school year. When it came time for me to move into my new dorm, I was feeling a little uneasy and my stomach was doing back flips. I felt like time was standing still, but once I had all my stuff unpacked I felt better. I felt better until I realized that Gloria, Sandy and Carol were living on the same floor as me.

When I found out I was so angry; I could not believe that those bitches were going to be on my floor. What kind of twist of fate was that? When they saw me, they tried to talk to me but I went into my room and closed the door. I did not want to see or speak to them, and fortunately, they respected that. I told myself eventually I would be able to put what happened behind me and until then I was going to have to stay strong. After a few minutes my mom gave me, a hug wished me good luck and then she left.

To help me feel even calmer and more centered I moved my stuff around my new room until I had everything exactly where I liked it. After I fixed up my room, I decided to write to Louisa and let her know that I got back to school unharmed. I really missed her but I knew that someday I would be able to go back to visit or maybe she could come visit me. Later on, that night there was a welcome back BBQ and a bonfire. I was so excited to be back at school with all my real friends. At the BBQ there were many delicious choices to choose from it was hard to choose which foods I wanted.

After I selected the food I wanted to eat, I sat at a table and ate my food. At the bonfire, I roasted marshmallows and caught up with some old friends of mine. I was having a great time, eventually my friends left but I decided to stay because I was having fun. Being at the bonfire was a blast and it was the perfect way to start the new semester and put mistakes of the past behind me.

As the night went on I saw Sandy, Gloria and Carol talking and pointing at me but I ignored them and started to walk back to my room. After I brushed my teeth and took a shower, I put my pajamas on and went to bed. As I lay in bed, I could not help but feel strange. I felt as if this was a dream and when I woke up, I would be back in England or at home with my mom. After thinking about this for a few minutes, I closed my eyes and fell asleep.

When I woke up in the morning, I discovered it had not been a dream and I had to hurry up or I was going to be late for class. I quickly got dressed brushed my teeth and hair, grabbed my books and headed off to class. After my classes were out for the day, I went to dinner and sat at a table by myself. After a few weeks of being back at Water

Crest College, I felt like my old self again I was not hurt or broken anymore and to me that was priceless.

I had a new routine that helped me get through every day and some supportive friends. I did not really trust the R.A.s so I kept my distance. They would try to talk to me but I would usually just give a quick response and then walk away. Sam was my R.A again but after everything, I had been through the year before I thought it was for the best that I keep my distance from him too.

Another thing that really helped me enjoy the school year was making some awesome new friends. My new friends Ryder Haven, Alexander Sillerson, Chester Wishers and Sarah Goddellerson were much cooler and nicer than anyone in my old friend group were. They were so accepting and nonjudgmental and I really was grateful for that.

Ryder was a rebel he did what he wanted and said what he wanted. He was also handsome with long wavy brown hair and piercing blue eyes. He was so handsome and cool that all the girls would drool over him. He was also charming and sweet I felt so lucky that he had chosen me to be his friend.

He was easy to talk to, and really cared about our friends and me. I always felt safe around him even when he was doing something that he knew would get him in trouble. Nothing scared him and I really admired that because I was scared of just about anything and everything. The two of us were quite a team and when our friends joined us, we were a crazy group. Even though all the cooler girls liked him and would constantly flirt with him, he ignored them and rolled his eyes at them. Every time I saw him, I felt my heart skip a few beats.

He was a rebel and would always recruit Alexander and Chester to help him pull pranks on people he did not like or agree with. Sarah and I never got involved with the pranks; we just hid them in our rooms when they asked us to. They would stay there until they felt it was safe to leave. I did not approve of this behavior but I cared about my friends so I always did my best to help them.

Alexander and Chester were kind of the followers of the group and Sarah and I were the peacemakers. My new friends were a great support system, I could tell them anything, and they would just listen without judgment and I would do the same for them. We became a strong inseparable group. It was as if we had been friends for our whole lives, instead of just a few weeks. Every day with them was an adventure, and I never knew what to expect.

One night I was hanging out with them, when I heard a knock on my door. I looked questioningly at Ryder thinking that they had played another prank but he just shrugged. Much to my surprise, it was my old friends at my door. I could not believe it; they had ignored me for days and now all of a sudden they wanted to talk. They gave me a sob story, about how Gloria ditched them for in her opinion more fun and sophisticated people.

I could not believe what I was hearing. This was so ludicrous it was almost comical; these women were the same people who spread lies about me and tried to get me sent home. After all that, they now wanted to be my best friends again. I wanted to laugh but I did not because I did not think it would be appropriate. I just stared at them and tried to think of something to say.

After ditching me because Gloria convinced them to spread lies about me, they expected me to forgive them as if nothing had happened. I took a deep breath and then said the following, "Look I am sorry that Gloria ditched you but honestly I don't ever want to see or talk to any of you."
"Gracie we're...
"Save it I don't want to hear it you really hurt and broke me in fact your lies almost got me sent home."
"You think that by coming here and fake apologizing and giving me a sob story is going to change how I feel?"
"No but we didn't mean to say those things, and we didn't intend for you to find out."
"Okay well that is neither here nor there. The facts are what they are, whether you meant for me to find out or not is irrelevant."
"I can't be your friend anymore I need positive people in my life, and that isn't you.

At this point, I started to get a little emotional so Sarah took over.
"I know I don't know any of you but I think you should leave."
"I do not know the whole story but I do know that you really hurt Gracie last semester."
"She needs and deserves a new start, and she isn't going to get one if she is friends with toxic people like you."
"Saying your sorry is a start but it doesn't change anything."

I smiled, thanked Sarah and then I made my last statement.

"Please get out of my room and don't ever come back. I have new friends now and I want to have a tranquil and enjoyable evening with them."

"I wish you the best but it would be for the best if you leave now."

After I said my parting words, it became clear to them that I no longer wished to be friends with them and they left. For the rest of the evening we just talked and listened to music. When my new friends left, I went to bed and I tried my best to get some sleep. As I slept I dreamed about my father and in the dream he told me was proud of me for removing toxic waste of space people like my ex friends from my life.

They hurt me and left me feeling hurt and broken and think they can just get away with it. What really made my blood boil is when it bit them in the ass they decided to come crying back to me and thought I would give them another chance. It felt good knowing that I had done the right thing and I could now enjoy my semester and focus on things that truly mattered.

The rest of that night, I thought about my choices and my future. I had a degree to earn and classes to pass. I was going to make that year my year and nothing was going to go wrong. If only I had been able to predict the future, I would have been able to save my friends and myself a lot of heartache and pain.

Eventually Ryder and I realized we loved each other

and we started going out. Alexander fell for Sarah so we became a couples group. Chester also found someone a ruggedly handsome man named James. After meeting James, he introduced us to his roommate Michael Dante. He was the protector of the group, and he was always bailing Ryder and the other three crazy men out of trouble. Each one of my friends were special to me and I loved them all, they were there for me and I was there for them. What I did not know was just how painful and hard our lives were about to get.

One dark and stormy night, one of Ryder's pranks went too far and things got out of control. This time the prank was against the fraternity boys. Ryder decided to send them chocolate chip cookies with chili powder on top and threw water balloons at them in front of the hottest sorority girls in school. Personally, I thought it was hilarious but the fraternity brothers were furious.

After the prank had occurred and they found out who had done it, they threatened to seek revenge on Ryder and the gang. After hearing that they threatened my boyfriend, I started to feel nervous and apprehensive. Ryder was my world and I could not bear the thought of something bad happening to him. Since I was feeling so apprehensive, I decided I had to do something, so I asked Michael what I should do. He smiled and told me he would make sure that no harm came to Ryder.

He advised Ryder to lay low until the fraternity forgot about what happened. Days past and nothing happened so, Ryder and I decided it would be safe for us to go out on a date. We went to the local Chinese restaurant, which had amazing food and a warm and inviting atmosphere. I was having a blast but while we were eating two of the people that had threatened Ryder, walked into the restaurant.

Before they could see us, we finished eating, paid our bill, and snuck out the back door. It was a starry night with the stars twinkling and the moon shinning and lighting up our path as we walked to my dorm. I was having a fabulous time walking home with Ryder but I still could not help but worry about the frat brothers.

When we arrived at my dorm, Ryder kissed me, and gave me a bear hug. Being in Ryder's arms made me feel so safe, for a moment all my worries went away. I was having so much fun I asked him to hang out with me in my room but Ryder told me that he had to meet up with the men for a walk and some manly fun whatever that meant. He walked me back to my dorm and kissed me goodnight. I can still remember the last things we said to each other.
"Goodnight Gracie I love you."
 "Goodnight Ryder I love you too, please be careful."
"I will be baby don't worry I will see you tomorrow."

After a few more minutes, Ryder left, and I walked into my dorm. I did not know it at the time but that was the last time I would see my boyfriend alive. I walked up the stairs and walked to my room. After brushing my teeth and changing into my pajamas, I went to bed but I was not asleep for long. A few hours later, I woke up due to hearing a loud knock at my door. I opened the door, there stood Sarah she was shaking, and had tears in her eyes.
"Sarah what is it, what's happened?

"Oh Gracie there's been a fight between the guys and the fraternity brothers.

"I'm so sorry to have to tell you this Gracie but one of our friends has been murdered."

"Oh my shit on a cracker which one?"

"Ryder".

I let out a scream and broke down in tears. Sarah pulled me into a hug and I screamed and cried into her shoulder. As I was crying, I could hear her crying and screaming too. We just stood there holding onto each other while crying and screaming. I knew that we were probably waking other residents up but as selfish, as it sounds at that moment I did not care.

I could feel my heart breaking in my chest and I thought for a split second that I was having a panic attack. My heart was pounding in my chest and I did not know what to do or what to say next. Eventually we let go of each other and we tried to calm down.

"Who told you what happened?

"Alexander called me from the police station. He and the rest of our guy friends are giving their statements to the police and then they are going to come here, they should be here soon."

"Holy shit on a cracker I can't believe this happened; I thought Ryder was going to be careful."

"They were Gracie the frat guys started the fight, Ryder, Alexander, Michael Chester and James were just hanging out when the frat guys attacked them."

Sarah and I tried to figure out what to do and how to

get through this rough time. As we were trying to figure things out I stated to think about what was going to happen to the group. I was not sure how but I knew we were going to have to keep our heads held high, and not let this tragedy ruin the rest of the semester and school year.

There were going to be dark days ahead but we were going to have to stay strong and stick together. A little while later, there was a knock at the door. Sarah went to answer it; I was hoping it was Michael, James, Chester and Alexander. However, it was Sam.
"Hey, Sarah, can I please speak to Gracie?"
"I'm sorry Sam but now is not a good time for you to talk to her. She is pretty upset and shaken up right now."
"I understand that but I need to talk to her it's important."

When I heard that I ran to the door and even though I was still crying and shaking, I decided I had to face Sam and tell him how I felt. I walked towards the door, took a deep breath, and opened my mouth to speak.
"Please go away Sam I can't talk right now."

I know that sounded stupid but that was all I could think of to say at the time.
"I'm sorry Gracie I'm so sorry, I never meant for this to happen."

I did not even know how to respond to that so I just stood there. After a few minutes of me standing there, I assumed would leave but he did not. Sam refused to leave he said he needed to explain some things. I told him if he did not get out of my room, I would call the police and tell them to take him out of my room. Eventually he got the message and left.

After Sam left, Sarah shut the door, walked over to me and gave me a hug. Eventually the boys, showed up a little while later, and held me while making soothing sounds to help me calm down. They sparred me the details of what happened because they figured it would be too painful for me to hear. Instead, they just kept hugging me and telling me it was going to be okay.

I wanted to believe them but I had serious doubts that things would ever be okay again. I saw things differently. I supposed most people see things differently after a tragedy. I felt like screaming but no words came out so I just let my friends keep hugging me. Once I was calm, they let me go and asked if I wanted them to stay with me for the night. I said yes, went to the bookshelf, grabbed the bear that Ryder had given me and got back into bed. I tried to sleep but I could not so I just laid there in the dark, in silence.

Later on in the morning, Sadie the area coordinator stopped by my room. Michael answered the door. He told her it was not a good time for me but she said she had questions to ask me. I went to the door and told her to go away I did not want to see anyone. She said she understood but I was going to have to talk to her. I told her I did not anything to say and then I asked her to go away and leave us alone and closed the door.

Fortunately, after that she got the message and left. After a few minutes went by Michael told me the person that had killed Ryder was in jail, and we were all going to have to speak when the case went to trial. I wasn't sure how I felt about speaking at the trial but if it meant helping ensure that the person who murdered Ryder got the sentence he deserved I was willing to try. I found out it was not Sam who murdered Ryder it was Christopher Wicks. The news of the arrest brought me some comfort but I still felt angry.

    I felt that Sam and the other clowns were just as responsible because they did not do anything to stop him. Later that day the news of Ryder's death spread through campus like a wildfire. We also found out because of Ryder's murder, the fraternity was going to be facing serious sanctions and fines. As for the men that were involved in the fight, they received probation for three years and had to do community service.

    I was fine with the punishment they received but none of it was going to bring Ryder back. A little while later, we found out Ryder's mom, dad and his little sister Bridget-Marie were on their way to come get his belongings. I felt sorry for them because I know how close Ryder had been to his family. A month before he died he had introduced me to them and they were very nice people. When we got back to the dorm, they were in his room.

    We told them we were sorry for their loss. They thanked us for our condolences, and Bridget gave me a box, and told me to open it later. When I asked her why she was giving it to me, she told me Ryder would want me to have it. After she gave me the box, we helped pack up Ryder's things and then they left. After the left, I opened the box and inside was a beautiful diamond ring. I cried he was planning to propose, even though we had only known each other for a little while. I put the ring on my finger and my friends gave me a hug. The hug helped but I still felt as if someone had ripped my heart out of my chest and chopped it up into tiny unrepairable pieces.

After a few minutes, I said goodbye to my friends, went back to my room, and did some cleaning. The cleaning helped take my mind off things for a while but once I was done, I could not help but think about what happened. The world was different to me now it appeared colder and less safe. After a few minutes went by, I called my mom and let her know what had happened. She asked me if I wanted to come home for the weekend and I said yes. She picked me up that evening and I got away for a little while. When I got home, I went straight to my room and closed my eyes for a while.

When I woke up my mom brought me up a tray of food, I ate every bite and then brought the tray downstairs. I enjoyed being home with my mom and my brother and taking a break from campus. It was nice getting a break from campus even if it was only for two days. While at home I hung out at my house, I did not call Millie or any of my friends from home because I was not up for company. My mom took me shopping and to the movies which helped but I was still depressed over Ryder's death. When I got back to school, there was a note taped to my door from Sam. I opened it and I still remember what it said.

Dear Gracie, I am sorry that you lost your boyfriend and I hope you do not blame me for his death. I was not even there when it happened, so how could I be at fault?

Anyways I hope you can understand that I had nothing to do with his murder. —Sam. After I read the note a few times I tore it up, threw the pieces in the trash, and texted my friends to let them know that I was back. They came to my room and filled me in on everything that had happened while I had been away. Everyone had been talking about the murder and me. My friends told me my former friends blamed me for Ryder's death.

    They did their best to defend me, which made me feel better, but I was still really hurt and angry. It was still hard for me to be able to digest everything that had just happened. It was as there was a dark cloud over my head and it was never going to go away. Later that night a memorial and candlelight vigil were held so that the students could honor Ryder's memory and to help people heal.

    When the memorial started, I could barely see because the tears in my eyes blurred my vision. When it came time for the candlelight vigil, we lit candles and placed them on the memorial the school made to honor Ryder. While we were there, I saw the R.As, some of them were crying, and I could not help but feel like they were crying crocodile tears. None of them liked Ryder so I strongly suspected that they just came to make themselves look good. I also saw my ex friends, but I tried to ignore them and focus on honoring the man I loved.

    A few minutes went by and they tried coming up to me but I just walked away. As I walked around, I saw Ryder's parents and younger sister. I walked over to say hello and see how they were doing. We talked for a while and then my friends joined us. After the Vigil was over Ryder's parents asked us to come to the funeral. The funeral was going to be a small gathering of family and friends to celebrate Ryder's life, and bring closure to his family and friends. They also asked me if I would speak at the service, I agreed even though I had no idea what I was going to say. I worked on that speech for days, until I finally came up with a speech worthy of Ryder.

When the day of the funeral came, I had a written speech in my hand and I was practicing it repeatedly in my mind. When it was my turn to speak, I said the following words

"We are all here today to honor a man that touched all of our lives and hearts. For me Ryder was my boyfriend but he was also my best friend. He was there for me at a time when I really needed someone and thanks to him, I found Sarah, Alexander, Chester, James and Michael. We should all remember him as the kind, funny and sweet person that we all knew and loved. Rest in Peace Ryder I love you."

After I said my speech, I broke down in tears. When the funeral was over my friends and I went back to school and hung out in Sarah's room. People were staring at us as we walked up the stairs but we ignored them. When we reached Sarah's room we closed the door, and we all started crying and held onto each other. What was really depressing was I did not even know whom I was crying for more myself, my friends or for Ryder.

I also felt jinxed first I lost my dad, and now I lost my boyfriend. After we stood there and sobbed for what seemed like forever, we went to my room and just talked for the rest of the night. I barely slept that night due to not being about to stop thinking about Ryder and how much I missed him and how I wished he was there with me. The next day we all received an email asking us to go to the conference room at The Lounge. We went to the conference room at the Lounge Center and saw that the fraternity brothers were waiting for us.

    When I saw them sitting there with smug looks on their faces I wanted to slap them, but I knew that would not solve anything so I refrained. Finally, the man that sent the email entered the room and sat down. Each member of the fraternity got up and read a letter they wrote to us apologizing to us for their actions. After listening to a few of them, I stood up, took a deep breath and said,
"Are you kidding me you think by reading letters that makes up for what happened?"
"You think by reading those letters changes the fact that, you all stood there while Christopher murdered my boyfriend in cold blood?"
"Do you guys even realize that because of your frat brother my best friend- boyfriend is dead?"
"If it wasn't for you Ryder would still be alive."
"You are terrible people and I will never forgive you for what you have done."

    After staring at everyone for a minute, I picked up my things and stormed out of the room. As I walked around to try to calm down I grew more and more angry. I could not believe that those idiots thought by reading some stupid letters I was going to forgive them for what happened to my boyfriend. My friends stayed and then went to find me.

When they found me, they gave me a bear hug and told me they were proud of me for speaking out and telling those bastards how I felt. I knew that Ryder pulled pranks on them and mocked them but he did not deserve to die. Due to the selfish actions of one of their frat brothers, a student was dead a student who had been a friend, a boyfriend but most importantly a loving son to two grieving parents and a loving brother to a grieving sister.

After the meeting, we ran into Sadie who asked to speak with us about Ryder. This time we talked to her and surprisingly talking to Sadie helped us feel better. She was kind and listened to what we had to say without judgment. After a few minutes, I started to cry and Sadie held my hand and told me it was okay and things were going to be okay.

I wanted to believe her but I doubted things would ever be okay again. A few weeks went by and eventually it was time to go home for the holidays. When it was time for me to go home, I was ready to go, and have a chance to have a break from the drama that had been going on at school. My family went to Pennsylvania for Christmas, we stayed there until New Year's Day and then we went home. Normally I was happy to be there but not that year. I felt somewhat depressed but after a while, I felt better, and spent some quality time with my family and friends.

They all kept asking me how I was feeling and I tried my best to give them an honest answer but I was not sure how I was doing. I just told myself that even though I was hurting right now, I would eventually be able to be okay again. It was just going to take some time and patience.

When the school break was over, my friends and I made a vow that, we were going to stick together no matter how tough or ugly things got. Supporting each other through this rough period was not always easy but we managed. Sometimes even though it had been awhile since Ryder's death, people would stare at us and whisper behind our backs.

Sometimes I was tempted to ask them what they were looking at, but always refrained because I knew it was not worth it. We tried to ignore them and hoped that things would die down soon. When it came time to celebrate my birthday we had a fun and low-key celebration. They threw me a huge party with cake, ice cream, pizza and presents.

When I blew out the candles, I was thinking about Ryder and that I wished he had been there with us. Right before I opened my last present Sam walked into the room. He had been avoiding my friends and me ever since Sarah and I kicked him out of my room so I was curious as to what he was doing. Since I did not want to be rude, I decided to be mature and let him have a piece of cake.

However, after he had his cake I was hoping he would leave. Even though I was hoping he would leave, he did not he stayed. I opened my last present and then he handed me a present. I opened it and inside the present, there was gold wrapped chocolate coins and other candies.

I thanked him for the thoughtful present, and then he left. After he left, we listened to some more music and then cleaned and wrapped up the party and went to bed.

A few weeks went by and then the Dean of Students had decided that I needed to go back to counseling at the health center, to help me deal with my grief. It actually helped having someone to talk to about this. Sarah, Michael, Chester and James were my best friends, but it felt nice to talk to someone else about what happened too. I started to make real progress and feel maybe not okay but slightly better.

One day that all changed. Somehow two of the resident assistants found my counseling file and took pictures of it and posted them on social media. When I saw the pictures, I was devastated and a little embarrassed because everyone who saw the picture knew my personal business. Fortunately, a few days later the photos vanished from the site and the resident assistants were fired and suspended from school for the remainder of the year. I was relieved about the punishment but I did not have much time to dwell on the matter because, because Christopher's trial was going to be starting soon.

News of the trial spread though the campus quickly many people came up to my friends and me and let us know that we were in their thoughts and prayers. It felt good to know that people cared about what we were going through but to be honest I just felt unsure about everything. A part of me felt like the trial was going to force me to relive some of the pain that I had been trying to forget about. It also was not as if putting the scumbag in jail was going to bring Ryder back. However, I also knew putting Christopher in jail would bring some sense of justice to us and to Ryder's family. I still did not know I was going to be able to face it but I knew I had to, for Ryder. He loved me, I loved him, and I was going to make sure that the bastard responsible for his death rotted in jail.

On the day of the trial, I hurried and got dressed because I was anxious to see what would happen. I was also feeling nervous about how the trial was going to go. Sarah and the others were waiting for me in Michael's car. I was just about finished getting ready when there was a knock on my door. I answered it figuring it was Sarah coming to tell me to hurry up.

Much to my surprise it was not Sarah or any of my friends, it was Janet one of the resident assistants. She and I had been close friends before I started dating Ryder but after I started dating Ryder, she stopped talking to me. I was astounded that she was there but I did not want to be rude, so I asked her what she wanted.

After a few seconds of awkward silence, she said to talk to me and check in. I was stunned and I wanted to ask her why she cared all of a sudden, but instead I told her I could not talk. I had to go to the trial for the murder of my boyfriend. She moved aside so I could leave my room, close, and lock my door. I started to walk away and head towards the stairs when she grabbed my arm.

After a few minutes, Sarah and the others showed up, pulled me away from her, and we left. As we were driving, I felt my stomach doing flip-flops I wanted to scream and cry but nothing came out, so I just sat there and hoped I could get through this. When we entered the courtroom, many people were there, including reporters. I tried to ignore them but they kept snapping pictures of us, until Ryder's mom asked them to stop.

When Christopher walked into the room with the guards, I wanted to strangle him with my bare hands. After the judge came in and we heard opening statements, it was time for witnesses to testify. The prosecution went first and I was the first witness. Even though I did not want to speak, I took a deep breath, walked up to the witness stand, and swore that the testimony I was about to give was the whole truth and nothing but the truth.

"Miss. Paris for the record, why are you here in this courtroom today?"

"I am here for one reason and one reason only, to bring the man responsible for killing my boyfriend Ryder Haven to justice."

"Do you recognize the man who is accused of killing Ryder Haven?"

"Yes I do we attend the same college."

After the prosecutor asked me some more questions, it was time for the defense attorney to question me.

"Ms. Paris for the court record, where were you when the fight or "attack" happened?"

"I was asleep in my dorm room."

"I didn't know about the attack until my friend Sarah woke me up to tell me what happened."

"I see, what had you been doing before you went to bed that evening?"

"Objection relevance?"

"I'm just trying to understand what happened that night."

"Overruled Ms. Pairs please answer the question.

"Ryder and I had gone on a date to a local restaurant. We were just finishing our dinner when we saw some of the frat brothers at the restaurant, so we left."

"Why did you leave the restaurant when you saw them, did they say anything or do anything that appeared threating to you?"

"No but before that night they threatened Ryder's life and we were concerned about our safety."

"I see, and yet you weren't concerned enough to stay with your boyfriend?"

"Objection."

"Your honor I am just asking why Ms. Paris hadn't stayed with Mr. Haven if she was so worried about his safety."

"Overruled but please get to the point counselor."

"Ms. Paris what caused you to think it was safe to go into your dorm room instead of staying with your boyfriend?"

"I didn't stay with him because he told me he had guy stuff to do with the guys and had promised me he would be careful."

"I thought they would be safe I didn't know that the fraternity brothers were planning on ambushing them."

"Here's a thought maybe instead of asking what I could have done to stop this tragedy from happening, you should ask your client's thug friends why they didn't stop it."

"Maybe instead of accusing me of being a neglectful girlfriend, you should ask why your client and his thug

friends ambushed my friends and murdered my boyfriend."
"Ms. Paris please try to control yourself, council do you have any more questions for this witness?"
"No your honor."
"Thank you Ms. Paris you may step down now."

After I walked away from the witness stand, I walked back to my seat put my head in my hands and tried to calm down. I had not meant to get so defensive but the defense attorney was an asshole. I loved Ryder and I would have done anything to protect him but he had said he would be careful. None of us knew that the fraternity thugs were going to attack the guys that night. After giving my testimony, it was my friends' turn to testify. The hardest to hear was Michael's testimony.

The details of that night were graphic, heart wrenching, and made the hairs on the back of my neck stand up. According to Michael, they were just walking around the town talking and joking around when they reached the pharmacy that is when the altercation started. Christopher and his friends started the altercation by calling the boys out. Within a few minutes of the altercation, starting fists were flying. After a few minutes, the fight seemed to stop.

Even though the fists were not flying, the fight continued. Michael and the others were trying to walk away but before they could Christopher pulled out his knife and stabbed Ryder twenty-seven times. After the final stab Ryder, fell down and collapsed in Michael's arms. Michael tried everything he could think of to save Ryder's life and called 911. As he was calling for help, the fraternity brother ran away like cowards. They knew what their brother had done and instead of facing the consequences, they left the scene. They let my boyfriend die they could have done something and they did nothing.

However, when the paramedics arrived it was too late Ryder was dead. He died in Michael's arms. Apparently his last words were look after my parents, my sister, Gracie and the group. Hearing Ryder's last words was the most painful part to hear. When I heard that I cried, Sarah put an arm around my shoulder and the boys held my hands. I wanted to scream but I did not instead I just held my breath and waited for the defense team to tell their side of the story. Then we heard the defense's side. The defense's side was maybe even harder to hear then Michael's testimony.

The defensive legal team had all the fraternity brothers speak. They said that Ryder had started the fight not the other way around. When I heard that, I wanted to jump up and kick the defense lawyer in the nuts. I started to stand up to say something, but Sarah grabbed my arm, gently pushed me back down and told me to control myself. I took a deep breath and tried my best not to react to the rest of the trial. As I sat there and heard the defense's side of what took place I started to feel like my stomach was on fire. I tried my best to stay calm and not let my emotions get the best of me.

I am not sure how relevant this was, but during one of their testimonies, they said that Christopher killed Ryder because he was not good enough for me. However, that was not the only reason that he killed Ryder, he also killed him so that Sam could date me. Apparently, in their eyes Sam was a much better boyfriend for me because he was smart and had a lot to offer a charismatic, intelligent and attractive girl like me.

When I heard that, I was stunned I did not even know that Sam liked me that way. I also felt furious that these men felt like they had the right to say whom I could and could not date. They had only known me for a few weeks. Did only knowing me for a few weeks suddenly make them the experts on who was or was not good enough for me? I did not think so, and a part of me wanted to march over there and strangle them with my bare hands. However, since we were in a courtroom, I knew I had to control myself.

The next person to speak for the defense was Wilber Wisherfield the III. He was a cocky arrogant toe rag and Christopher's best friend. I was eager to hear what he had to say because so far none of the defense's testimony was making sense to me. After taking the stand, Wilber said Sam had been in love with me since the day he met me. He said that Sam was obsessed with me and .always talked about how intelligent and enchanting I was. When I heard that I became even more livid then I already was, this punk was lying on the stand. None of what he was saying was making sense because when Sam met me he was dating Marcia Pasterson. However, after I thought about it for a second it made sense.

Shortly after Sam met me, Marcia dumped him after they had a very loud fight in the cafeteria. After everyone found out about the breakup, Marcia told everyone that he had feelings for a woman in the freshman class. When I found out about this, I assumed it was Kayla Wiskerson because he was always flirting with her and teasing her.

After we heard all of their testimonies and the closing statements from both sides, the jury went back to a room to decide the verdict. Time seemed to stand still in the courtroom and as every second passed, I tried to hold my breath and stay calm. After what seemed like hours, the judge announced that the jury was going to come back in and deliver the verdict.

Before we found out what the verdict was, going to be my heart was pounding in my chest. As the minutes passed, I thought I was going to pass out. When the jury came back in the judge asked for a verdict.
"After hours of deliberation we the jury find the defendant guilty of first-degree murder."

After the verdict judge asked for a 10-minute recess so he could figure out the sentence. After the recess, the judge gave Christopher a prison sentence of life imprisonment without the possibility of parole. When I heard the verdict and the sentence, I started crying but this time it was tears of joy. I looked at my friends and saw that they were crying too. At last, we could all start to heal and try to put this tragedy behind us.

I was not over it but at least we got justice and the peace of mind that this bastard was not going to be able to do that to anyone else. Even though I got the verdict, I wanted I still felt strange. I still thought the other fraternity brothers deserved some punishment. All they got for their part of the fight was a few months of community service, fines and probation.

I did not agree with the punishment I thought they should have received jail time but the only thing I could do was move forward. I told myself the most important thing for me to do now was stay focused on my future. A terrible thing happened but I could not let that event affect my whole year. I also made a vow that I was not ever going to let anyone else hurt those I loved or me ever again. I know that it seems silly to do that but it made me feel better at the time.

After the trial was over my friends and I walked out of the courtroom with our heads held high. As we were leaving the courthouse, I saw Ryder's parents and his sister and they came up to us and thanked us for our bravery. I did not think what we had done was so brave but I just went with it, gave them each a hug and then my friends started to leave. As we turned to leave reporters were hounding us, but we did not speak to them. Honestly, I think we were all speechless and no words came to mind.

Even though we got the verdict, we wanted; I still could not really make sense of what happened. As the day went on, I could not help but feel confused. If Christopher had murdered my boyfriend as a favor to Sam, then why did Sam not tell me how he felt? He had plenty of opportunities and he never once told me. None of this was making any sense, and I was trying to figure out what was true and what was not true. I was feeling extremely confused and hurt the guilty verdict did make me feel slightly better but it did not help my grieving.

I felt that there was a hole in my heart and nothing was ever going to fill it. I knew that I was going to be in for a long road of healing ahead of me but I also knew with time I would be ok. I was not sure if I was ready to deal with it but it helped knowing I had friends by my side that were going through the same thing. I knew we were all going to stick together and help each other through this rough time in our lives.

When we got back to school, everyone was staring at us. We just ignored them and went to my room. After an hour or two went by, we went to the cafeteria to get something to eat. We ate outside so we could have some privacy. Everyone looked at me and asked me if I was ok. I told them I was not ok and I was not sure if I would ever really be okay again. My friends gave me a hug and told me that it was going to take time, but eventually I would be okay again. As we were talking my ex friends showed up and sat at the table near ours but we ignored them.

They tried talking to us, but we just pretended we did not hear them and decided to leave. We grabbed our stuff, put the plates on the conveyer belt and left the cafeteria. As we were walking, I looked back and saw my former friends following us. I refrained from telling them to get lost because I did not want to be rude. I just ignored them and kept walking towards my dorm with my real friends. They followed us into the building and up the stairs, but I assumed it was to go to Sandy's room.

After realizing that I had, no desire to talk to them my former friends left us alone. Finally, we got to my door my friends moved aside so I could open my door. When we got into my room my friends and I sat on the beds, and I started to feel afraid. I was afraid of my future without Ryder. He protected me, and I could not even protect him.

For a split second, I felt that maybe the defense attorney was right. Maybe I should have stayed with Ryder. When I suggested that theory however, Michael told me that if I had been there Christopher probably would have killed me too. He told me and the others agreed that the only one responsible for Ryder's death was Christopher. Christopher was a sociopath he did not have any feelings or show any signs of remorse for what he had done.

Later on that night, my friends decided to spend the night because it was so late and because they did not want to leave me alone with my thoughts. When I woke up the next morning, my friends asked me if I wanted to go to breakfast but I told them no thanks. I just wanted to say in bed and try to sleep some more. I did not want to deal with anyone else; I just wanted to lay down and go to sleep.

My friends decided to go to breakfast and they promised they would bring something back for me. I felt lucky to have such kind and supportive friends.

We were a team and we would need to be a team even more when some of the fraternity brothers kidnapped Sarah and me. We were walking to the convenient store to buy some snacks and soda. Everything seemed normal. In fact we were having a great time walking, talking and laughing. However, when we walked up to the store, they jumped us, knocked us out, tied us up and dragged us to the old abandoned frat house. When we woke up, we were in an old bedroom tied to the beds. The room smelled like rotten old wood and dust. It was so bad it made me nauseous and dizzy.

As we looked around, we tried to stay calm and not show any emotions. My heart was racing and I could feel it pounding in my chest. After a few minutes, Sarah and I looked at each other with tears in our eyes. We could not speak any words but we did not have to we both knew what the other was thinking. We thought we were going to die in that awful place. They had taken our phones and placed them on a shelf so we could not reach them.

Since we were unable to reach our phones, we went to sleep. I hoped when I woke up it would be a dream but it was not. When we woke up the ugly bastards looked at us and smiled. They had us right where they wanted us and they knew it. For three days, we stayed in that smelly old house. Each day they fed us bread and soda crackers and gave us bottled water to drink. One night after consuming tons of alcohol, the ugly bastards were sound asleep on beds and a pullout couch.

As I watched them, sleep I knew that this was our only chance. I waited and silently hoped that the boys were on their way to save us. Suddenly I saw James, Michael, Alexander and Chester enter the room. I wanted to scream but nothing came out so I just smiled at them. A few minutes later Sarah noticed them too and they told us to come with them. When I saw the men friends standing there I was so relieved that I wanted to scream for joy Even though I wanted to scream I knew I couldn't because if I did then the boys would probably get tied up too or worse so I stayed quiet.

James untied us and told us to hurry up before the big losers woke up. Once we were, freed Sarah and I grabbed our phones and tried to walk out as quickly and quietly as possible. Unfortunately, for us one of the assholes woke up and saw us, which forced us to have to run for our lives. We ran and ran until we saw the car. Chester unlocked the car; we quickly jumped in the car and managed to get away.

We parked the car in the parking lot and then headed to my room where we stayed the rest of the night. At around three am, I heard a knock on the door but I did not answer it. After everything Sarah and I had just been through, I was not going to take any chances. For the rest of the night I stayed awake and made sure that no one bothered us. I tried to sleep but I was afraid to close my eyes because I did not want to end up back in the smelly old frat house.

The next few weeks went by in a blur. Sarah and I started to worry about our safety so when it got dark out we made sure we stuck together and walked where it was well lite. However, during the day we could do whatever we wanted because those people were not dumb enough to try anything in broad daylight. However, even though they did not try anything, we knew they were not going to stop.

Every night if I had to go out somewhere, I carried perfume in my purse so that I could defend myself with it. Michael told me while he thought the perfume idea was a good one, it would be better if I carried mace or pepper spray. One night when I had to go out to the store to buy some hygiene products, he gave me a can of each and told me to use it in an emergency. I thanked him and managed to walk to the store, buy what I needed and leave the store to go back to my dorm without any incidents. Later that night I made sure to lock my door and keep my pepper spray and mace with me at all times just in case I needed it.

One day while we were eating dinner at the dining hall, some other students overheard us talking about what happened and asked us why we did not go to the police. I did not know what to say and a part of me wanted to tell them to mind their own business but I did not. Instead, I told them we just wanted to keep it quiet and not make things worse and asked them to keep it to themselves. Eventually after promising that if anything else happened I would go to the police; I was able to convince them not to say anything.

Looking back, I wish we had told the police. If we had maybe, some of the other crazy stuff that happened would not have happened. One night about a week after the first attack, they tried to attack us again. Later that same evening after supper we decided to go back to my room and hang out for a little while. We were all having fun in my room until we heard a knock on the door. Instead of asking who was there, I just opened the door and saw that it was two fraternity hoodlums.

After pushing me aside, they forced themselves into my room. One of them grabbed me by my hair and pulled me out of the room. Fortunately, Sarah grabbed the can of mace from my storage closet and, held it up to him. While she held the mace in her hand, she told him if he did not let me go, she would spray him with it. He just laughed and dared her to try to spray it at him. Hearing this asshole make fun of my best friend really pissed me off. Before she could spray the mace at the hoodlum, I swung my head back and hit his nose. After screaming a few profanities, he let me go and Sarah put the mace back in my closet. While all of that commotion was happening, Michael called campus security.

When the officers arrived, they arrested the fraternity brats, and gave the one ice for his nose, which luckily for him was not broken just bruised. After the frat boys went to jail, the other security officer told us we would have to go to the security office so that we could give statements. After we had arrived at the security office and given our statements, we finally felt safe again.

They could no longer bother my friends or me ever again. After we got back from the security office, we ran into Sam who apologized for their behavior and told us he was sorry for everything that had happened during the school year. He said the fraternity was finished and those who had been harassing and bullying us were facing severe disciplinary actions. Sam also told me that the fraternity lied when they said that he was in love with me, he did care about me but as a friend. I was relieved that the frat brothers were facing severe consequences and that Sam had not been in love with me.

After we finished talking to Sam, we decided to celebrate. We went back to my room and had a party that lasted the rest of the night. The next day after I got out of my classes and finished my homework, I went to my room because I needed time to myself to digest everything. After everything that had happened over the past few weeks, I realized that I really needed to take a step back and breathe.

After a while, I was getting hungry so I went to the café to get some food. On my way there, I unfortunately ran into Janet Winds the last person I wanted to see right then. I walked past her without saying a word and then headed to the café. However, she followed me and after I got my food, she followed me to a table.

"Gracie please just hear me out, I really need to talk to you."
"Look Janet I really can't handle anymore confrontation right now. The past few weeks have been an emotional roller coaster."
"I wasn't going to confront you I just want to make sure that you're okay."
"Oh okay thanks I guess all things considered I am okay and a lot stronger then I realized."
"I miss Ryder a lot but I think eventually I will be able to feel like my old self again."
"Look Gracie, I am sorry Ryder died and that I acted all weird after you started dating Ryder, I always thought he was a weirdo but I guess he really loved you."
"It's okay, I am not angry anymore but thank you for the apology I appreciate it."
"I loved Ryder he was special and he loved me for me, he didn't try to change me."
"When I needed to talk he listened he didn't judge me and I

did the same for him."

"It sounds like you were pretty lucky to have each other but you know Gracie as long as you keep him in your heart and memories you will never lose him."

"I know thanks Janet and thanks for checking on me."

"Of course and anytime you need to talk I will be there for you."

After a few minutes, Janet hugged me and then she left. It felt good making peace with Janet. I knew it was not her fault that Ryder was dead. In that moment, I realized there was only one person to blame for losing Ryder and he was in jail. I also knew that it was a waste of time to hold on to the pain and anger. Making peace with Janet was the right thing to do.

The next day we found out that the fraternity men who had been harassing us were facing explosion and jail time and between you and me, that was the biggest victory of all. After we heard the news, my friends and I went to the mall for some retail therapy. After hanging out with my friends for a while we went back to school. After hanging out with my friends some, more I went to my room. This had been a very turbulent year and I had several emotions swirling around of me so I thought I should sort through them in private.

After a few hours, I felt better and decided to watch movies on my laptop. I still missed Ryder but it was not as painful anymore. I thought I would always miss him and love him but that was okay. It is okay to feel hurt and melancholic when someone you love dies but one thing that helps is that eventually the pain ends and the healing begins. Eventually I was able to fall asleep and get some rest.

The next day I decided to hangout in my room alone because I needed a day to myself. I told my friends I needed to be alone for the day. Fortunately, they respected my wishes. However not everyone respected my wishes. It was late in the evening and I was having a nice relaxing evening all by myself until I heard a knock on the door. I tried to ignore it but then I heard voices. I recognized them immediately as Bert Honeydew and Ryan Batterson. They were two R.As that everyone hated because they were really obnoxious and egotistical. I started to walk towards the door but then I stopped in my tacks, walked back to my bed, and closed my eyes.

"Gracie come on open the door."

When they did not get a response, they told me they were keying into my room. I did not respond I just keep my eyes closed and hoped they would go away. When my door opened, they walked over to me and started to shake me. When I woke up, I decided I was going to have to be nice but firm with these people so that they would leave me alone.

"Hello, Bert and Ryan, it is nice to see you but please leave me alone I have nothing to say to you."

"Gracie look we are sorry for your loss but it wasn't our fault."

I felt stunned when I heard that, I had never said that it was their fault or any of the residential life staff's fault. Since I did not want to be rude, I decided to be gracious.

"Thank you for your condolences, and I know it wasn't your fault."

"There is only one person responsible for this tragedy, and the good news is that he is in jail and will be in jail for the rest of his life."

"Gracie…"

"Look I don't want to be rude, but I am really not up for company right now."

"I have been through a lot and I just need some time and space to deal with this on my own." They looked at me and then left closing my door behind them.

After they left, I started t to feel better and decided to go for a walk at the river. I had not been there all year but for some reason that night seemed like the perfect night to go. When I arrived at my special spot, I sat on the rock and looked at the little island and the moon. I started to feel like my old self again, which scared me a little bit. I did not want to go back to being the morose loner woman I was a year ago.

As I sat there, I thought about everything that had happened to me and to the people I loved that year. I also thought how I was going to move forward and not let past mistakes or ignorant heartless people ruin the remaining years I was going to spend at school.

After a few hours, I headed back to my room, got ready for bed, and tried to get some sleep. For the rest of the year, I spent my time hanging out with friends and working hard in all my classes. The end of that year came before I knew it.

On the last day, I had to say goodbye to Sam because

he was graduating. When I went to say goodbye to him we both laughed said we were sorry, wished each other well and said goodbye. Saying goodbye to Sam was probably one of the hardest things I have ever had to do. He had been a good friend to me even though at times I doubted him.

After saying my goodbyes to Sam and my friends, I went back to my room to pack up my belongings. As I was going through my stuff, I found an old love note from Ryder. As I read it I all my feelings from that day returned. Since I did not want to lose it, I put it in a box with the rest of the things that Ryder gave me and decided that I would keep it in a special place in my room at home.

When I got back home, I decided I was going to enjoy my summer. I was not going to let the unfortunate events that had taken place during the school year ruin my summer. I decided inside of feeling sorry for myself I was going to have fun. That summer was amazing and I had a blast. Every day I went on a different adventure. For the first time since losing Ryder I felt content and blissful and starting enjoying my life again. It felt good being back in RI and being around all the places and people that meant the world to me. Spending time at home was just the break I needed after such a wild and crazy school year.

Most of the days were peaceful and quiet while others were busy and loud. I still thought about Ryder but I thought about all the memories not just the fact that he died. I was also relieved to be home because at home I did not have to deal with people asking me if I was okay 20-35 times a day. I know people meant well but it was getting exhausting telling everyone that I was fine all the time.

After a few weeks at home, I received my final grades and I had done really well I received three A's and one B. When I showed my mom my grades, she was proud of me and took me out for a special dinner to celebrate. It was just the two of us since my brother had to work but I did not mind. It was nice spending one on one time with my mom.

When my brother came home, he saw my grades and he said he was also proud of me. I thanked him and then he insisted on taking me out for ice cream. After our ice cream, we went home, and watched television together. As I sat there, I could not help but feel loved and safe.

As the summer went on, I started to feel like this was the best thing I could have done for myself. While at home, I could just relax and hang out with my family and friends in Rhode Island. I was so relieved to be home, that I did not know what else to say. Nothing seemed to matter I was home and I did not have to think about school. I missed my friends but I could not wait to see what this summer had to bring, and for the first time in a long time, I felt safe.

One day as I was leaving the library to walk home, I ran into Mr. Gibson. At first, I did not know what to do, so I just decided to walk away. He tried to talk to me but I just kept walking I did not have anything to say to that low life. He actually followed me for a little while until I reached my neighborhood. As I walked around my neighborhood, I decided to turn around and make sure he was not behind me. Fortunately, he was no longer behind me so I continued to walk until I finally reached my house. When I got inside my house, I called my mom to let her know I was home and then I went into the kitchen to make a snack.

Suddenly I heard our doorbell so I went to see who was at the door. When I saw, who was at the door my heart sank because it was Mr. Gibson. I opened the door and told him to leave or I was going to call the cops. He dared me to call them so I dialed 911 and I held it up to him to show him that I was serious.

He told me to hear him out but I told him to leave and made it clear that I was not afraid to hit send. He left but not before telling me, he was going to come back another day when I was ready to hear what he had to say. I could not believe how ignorant and stupid a man who called himself a teacher was being. I told him not to bother because I never wanted to see or speak to him again and then I slammed and locked the door. A few weeks went by, and he came back this time my brother Jason was home with me.

Since I was upstairs, cleaning my room Jason answered the door. Mr. Gibson started to introduce himself but Jason told him he knew exactly who he was and told him to get lost. Fortunately, he got the message and never came back. The rest of that summer went by fast but it was a lot of fun. I went on many day trips with my family and friends and really enjoyed myself. Even though I was having fun, I knew that eventually I was going to have to go back to school.

Unfortunately, before I left Millie and I had a huge fight and decided to end our friendship. We were at a local ice cream shop and I thought we were having a great time. I could tell there was something on Millie's mind and was hoping she would just tell me what was going on

"Gracie I'm sorry but I can't be your friend anymore, you are just nonstop drama and I need to step away from it right now."

"Okay that's fine just remember not to call me the next time there is drama in your life because I won't answer."

"Don't worry I won't, I have my sister I don't need you."

After hearing that I felt hurt and betrayed but since I did not want to make a scene, I threw out my empty cup from my ice cream, pushed my chair in and walked away. Millie called after me but I did not stop or turn around. I was done with her and done dealing with people who did not want me in their life anymore.

As the summer ended, I felt relieved that I was leaving and going back to New Hampshire not because I did not love RI but I was ready to go and see what this year had to offer. Before I knew, it was time for school to start again. The following year started great and I was excited to be back on campus. My friends and I lived suite in North dorm so that we could all live together. I went to my classes, hung out with my friends and went to counseling. I also had two other friends join the group. It was not all fun and games there was one ongoing problem that caused a lot of stress and drama. The two new friends Molly and Amy-Ann fought constantly. It was actually stressful to be around them.

It did not matter where we were or what we were doing, they always had to have a go at each other. We figured out that the only way to avoid this and avoid going completely insane, was we had to make excuses as to why we could not hang out with them. Making excuses worked for a while but eventually it stopped working.

I was starting to feel stressed out so I went to the health center and talked to Mary who was my therapist about it. Mary always listened to what I had to say and I always felt better after talking to her. After hearing me talk about this for weeks, she told me I needed to tell them how their constant bickering made us feel.

I always said that I was afraid that they would get mad at us, or they would use us as a way to keep arguing with each other. The last time we were studying together in the room, they had a huge fight and two resident assistants had to come and investigate due to one of our neighbors complaining about the noise. I have never been more embarrassed I just wanted to sink into the floor and so did Sarah.

When I answered the door after hearing the annoying knocking on the door there stood Chris and Gram. I let them into our room and they told Molly and Amy-Ann that they had to leave because they wanted to talk to Sarah and me alone. They had Sarah and I come back to the duty office with them to talk about it. They asked us why we and our other friends put up with all this fighting and never saying how we felt about it.

I told them because I was not sure Molly and Amy-Ann would listen to me or they would just use what I say to keep arguing. Sarah agreed with me, and she felt embarrassed by the fighting. Chris smiled and said that if they were really our friends then they would listen. We talked for a little longer and then we felt better so we decided to go back to the room. We put pajamas on, hopped into bed, and went to sleep. The next morning, we woke up to the sun shining through our window and a nice brand-new day ahead of us.

Molly texted me and asked if Sarah, Chester, Alexander, James, Michael and I would go to brunch with her since her and Amy-Ann were still fighting. I responded with no thanks we were busy and did not want to deal with the fighting that I knew was bound to happen. I felt proud of my decision until I received a response text from Molly. Molly was furious and said hurtful things that broke my heart but I did not let them bother me.

I cried a little but I was also proud of myself for standing up for myself and for my friends. Eventually it was time for dinner so we walked to the cafeteria. As we were walking, I wondered what the food options were going to be that night. When we arrived at the cafeteria, we sat at our usual table and hoped for no drama. Once Amy-Ann and Molly walked into the cafeteria, I knew then that something was about to go down and I was not looking forward to what it was going to be. They sat together which really shocked me because I thought they were still fighting.

They stared at us; we just ignored them and left. We decided to go back to my room and watch movies and relax. When we arrived at my room, we all kept getting phone calls from them but we ignored them. I was so tired of the drama I was willing to do anything to get some peace and quiet for a while. We watched a few movies and then my friends left and I went to bed. It was hard avoiding Amy-Ann and Molly but we did not have a choice, because to be honest I could not handle any more of their constant squabbling and bickering anymore.

The group and I stuck together and made things as pleasant as possible, we tried to make everyday fun because it was pointless in dwelling on what we had no control over. However, despite all the fun times there was still some trouble brewing. Amy-Ann and Molly were still determined to be in our lives. They tried to convince us that they would not fight anymore, but I still had some doubts.

We took a vote and decided to believe them, which turned out to be a mistake. About a few weeks after the vote, Amy Ann and Molly were fighting again. This time it was over a boy that they both really liked. His name was William Boxthorn and he was cute at least according to Molly and Amy-Ann. I thought he was creepy and weirdly cocky. He was always showing off his fancy car and expensive clothes.

Eventually they decide that neither of them would go out with William, which turned out to be a good solution and brought some peace to our group. There was only one problem he really liked me but I was not ready for a serious relationship with another man. When I told William how I felt, he started stalking me and Molly and Amy-Ann refused to speak to me. The rest of the group took my side because they knew I had told William that I was not ready to date anyone yet.

Unfortunately having Molly and Amy Ann not

speaking to me was the least of my problems. William would follow me around all day every day. Wherever I went, William was not too far behind me.

At first, I was able to just ignore him and not pay attention to him. Unfortunately, that did not stop him from paying attention and making unwanted advances towards me. He was determined to go out with me whether I wanted to go out with him or not. Eventually Amy-Ann and Molly figured out that I did not want to go out with William and they decided to help me get him to leave me alone.

We assumed that if I stopped paying attention to him he would get the message and leave me alone, and for a few weeks, it appeared that he got message and moved on to someone else. He was dating this girl name Vanessa for a while but then after a few weeks, they broke up and he went back to stalking me

He also started sending me expensive gifts. I would return the gifts to him but that did not stop him from sending them. Another thing he would do was every day when my friends and I would go to the dining hall, we would still at our usual table and even if no one would talk to him; he would sit there with us. We even tried asking him to leave me alone but that did not work either.

Feeling a little frustrated I decided to take a break from eating at the dining hall for a while. I went to the small grocery store that was just up the road from my school and bought a month's worth of groceries. It was a little expensive but it beat me having to deal with unwanted attention from William. In my absence, William did not sit at the table but he did stare at the table to see if I had shown up. Some people began to ask me why I did not just tell campus security about what was going on if it bothered me so much. I always told that that a part of me felt sorry for William. I did not think he fully understood that when a girl said no she meant no. After putting up with William's behavior for months, my friends decided to go to campus security and tell them what was going on.

    I was a little livid at first but then I realized they were only trying to help. They just wanted me to be able to eat my meals with them in the cafeteria in peace, which is what I wanted too. The officers at campus security were very nice and helped me come up with a solution so that I would not have to worry about William stalking me every day. Campus security put together a rule that stated that William could not be anywhere near me anymore. I felt a little better but I was worried about how William was going to react. I did not want any more drama, however; I knew that the shit-storm was just starting it was not going to blow over anytime soon.

    When I went to dinner later that night, I felt a little apprehensive about being in the same room as William. However, as my friends put it, I was going to have to deal with this eventually. We sat down at the table and just started talking and laughing about random things, it felt like old times before I had met William. For a second I thought that I felt as if Ryder was right there with me, which made me feel safe, that is until I saw William. At first, I thought he was going to sit with us but he turned away and sat at an empty table. A part of me felt guilty however, I just ignored it.

    I had been honest with him and he chose not to listen. The rest of the time at the dining hall was fun. We all laughed until our faces hurt. For the first time in a long time, I was smiling, laughing and having fun with my friends. When we got up to leave, William was glaring at us but we did not care. We just ignored him and kept on walking. When we got back to our dorm, my friends and I decided to have a party just for the heck of it. However, as we were getting everything ready something happened that none of us expected.

    I was just putting the chips and salsa out when suddenly I heard a loud banging sound outside the door of our suite. Since everyone else was busy, I answered the door. When I answered the door there stood William with my favorite flowers and a card. I did not know what to say or do. I just stood there like an idiot until Sarah came to the door and told William to go away and then she tried to close the door.

    However, William forced it open and told me that if I did not at least go on one lousy date with him, he would kill himself. He also showed me the gun that he intended to use. Sarah screamed and the rest of the group and a few other students came running and called 911.

    William fired the gun and it hit me in the shoulder. I screamed in pain and passed out but once, the EMTs arrived and took me to the hospital. Sarah went with me and held my hands.

    William went to the hospital too but to the psychiatric wing. He was going to stay there so that he could get some help. As for me, I had to stay in the hospital for a while but eventually I recovered and went back to school. When I came back, I was not sure how the other students would treat me. However, I decided not to care, I was better and I was relieved. William had to stay at a psychiatric hospital for observation.

I kept wondering if he would return and I would have to deal with him. When I asked my friends about him, they told me he was expelled and last they heard was seeking treatment at a psychiatric hospital in his hometown. When I found out he was expelled I felt sorry for him but then I realized it was not my fault. I had told him how I felt and he still pursued me. I knew he was not a terrible person he just needed some mental health help and now he was going to get it. I also felt relieved that I was not going to have to worry about him bothering us anymore. My friends and I did not discuss William again after that because we all agreed it was better not to dwell on the subject. It was better to focus on enjoying the remainder of the school year.

Eventually it was time to celebrate my twenty first birthday. My friends and I called a cab and they took me on a bar crawl and we had a blast. At the end of the night, we called a cab and we all got in and went back to school.

The rest of that year was pretty peaceful and quiet. I did not mind because after all the crazy events that had happened it was nice to have some quiet time. I did well in my classes and ended up getting straight A's in all my classes. On the last night of school, my friends and I celebrated with a party that lasted until early in the morning. After the party, we cleaned up and went our separate ways.

When summer vacation time came I spent time healing and hanging out with my family. I also went to the mall with my friends and met up with my old friend Angelo. He looked the same and was as charming as ever. It felt good to be home with my friends and family again after a crazy year of school. One day my mom decided it was time for a mother daughter beach and lunch day. My brother was at work so it was perfect because after such a turbulent school year, I needed some beach therapy. When we arrived at the beach, I saw Millie and her family but I just ignored them. They were not worth my time if Millie did not want me in her life then I did not want her in mine either.

After we found our spot, I put on sunscreen and headed for the water. I loved being at the beach it did not matter how hot or cold it was I loved being there. There was something therapeutic and relaxing about the place. I do not know if it was the ocean or the sand but I always felt better after a day at the beach.

As I was swimming in the ocean I thought I heard Millie calling my name but I did not stop I just keep swimming until I was really far out. Unfortunately, I was a little too far out and had to swim for a while to get back to the shore again. My mom scolded me for the scare I gave her, but eventually she got over it.

After a few minutes, I reapplied my sunscreen and decided to read for a while. After a few hours at the beach, it was time for lunch. After lunch, my mom and I decided to head for home. I was so tired from my fun day at the beach

I fell asleep in the car. The rest of that summer, I hung with my family and my friends. For the upcoming school year, I just hoped and prayed it would be easy. I also hoped and prayed that nothing too wild or crazy would happen to my friends or me.

When school started back up again I was living in a double room with no roommate. My friends all got apartments but I wanted to live in the dorms. However, I was always welcome at my friends' apartments, which was nice. After I unpacked I met up with my friends, however we realized that two of our friends were missing. It turned out Molly and Amy- Ann had decided to transfer, which not going to lie made me a little disappointed but I was happy for them.

After a few weeks had gone by, I met another boy that I thought was perfect. We took it slow and started dating. His name was Astor Milks, he was nice and handsome but there was one problem with our relationship, his family hated me. After about three or so months of dating each other, Astor cheated on me.

I still remember what happed. I walked into the dining hall, got my food and then I saw what I hoped I would never see. I saw Astor making out with the biggest slut in school Sally Stanforberger. .I sat down at a table and just began eating my food; my friends joined me and all gently patted me on the back. Astor came over to the table but Chester and Michel told him to get lost. After we were finished eating we went to my room to purge it of all the things that reminded me of Astor.

After we finished cleaning up my room, I felt a little better. I think a part of me was still feeling a little humiliated that I had trusted that entitled asshole. After cleaning, we went to the coffee house, and unfortunately, Astor was there. Even though I was still wrathful at him for hurting me, I tried my best to ignore him. Michael asked me to play pool with him so I did. I was not a good player but Michael did not care he was kind and patient with me.

Playing pool with Michael and being with my friends was the best possible way for me to feel better. For the first time that day, I started laughing because I started to feel that things were going to be okay. I started to feel better and I was having a great time just hanging out with one of my close friends.

What I did not realize was Astor was watching us. When I looked over my shoulder and saw him glaring at us, we just ignored him and kept on having fun. Eventually we decided to leave because it was getting late, and we were all getting tired. We walked out of the coffee house and said goodnight.

When I got back to my room, I changed my clothes, brushed my hair and teeth and got into bed. As I pulled the covers back and tucked myself in, I heard knock on my door. Instead of answering it, I just ignored it and went to sleep. It felt good to be able to have a chance to get some rest. When I woke up the next morning, I had fifty text messages on my phone. Most of them were from my mom and my friends so I answered them. The other text messages were from Astor and surprisingly Astor's parents.

I was curious as to how they got my number but I deleted the texts without even reading them. I decided that I wanted to be alone so I just stayed in my room all day. I sent a text to my friends asking for some alone time, and surprisingly that worked and no one bothered me. I received the peace and quiet I needed which was nice. I watched movies and ate junk food. It was nice to have a chance to be by myself and think things through for a little while.

While I was thinking, I decided that the best thing to do was to keep; my head held high and not let Astor get to me. He was the one that did something wrong not me. I did not cheat or hurt him in any way. I also realized I was not just angry that he cheated, I was also angry because he showed no regard for our relationship or me. I truly loved him and it really hurt that he did not love me. Later on that day, my friends came over to check on me.

We just hung out and watched television on my flat screen TV that was in my room. It was nice being with my friends and relaxing. We had fun watching TV and laughing until our faces hurt but then I heard a knock on my door. Sarah opened it and when she did, I saw who was outside the door. As I looked at who was there, my heart sank it was Astor. Instead of letting, Astor in, I let Sarah close my door in his face. I did not want to see or hear what that two-timing weasel had to say.

He kept knocking but we did not let him in because we did not want him hanging out with us. Fortunately, eventually he got the message and left us alone. I felt somewhat guilty about not letting him in but then I reminded myself that he deserved it. He was a pathetic loser and I was better off without him. Astor and Sally deserved each other and I hoped they would be very content together. I know that sounds bitter diary but at the time that was how I felt. I had trusted this man and he let me down.

 Eventually my friends left and I was alone again but I did not mind, I liked being alone sometimes so I could think and hope that things would get better. After a few minutes, I decided to finish my homework and go to bed. While I was asleep for the first time in a while, I dreamt about Ryder. We were hanging out at all our favorite spots, and then the dream faded out into a dark cloudy mist.

 When I woke up, I went to brunch with my friends and I told them about my dream. They hugged me tight and told me everything was going to be fine. I wanted to believe them but I was not sure if things were going to be fine. After brunch I decided to do something I had not done in a while, I went to the river and just hung out by myself. Eventually my friends found me and decided I needed so time away from campus, so we drove around and did some intense retail therapy.

 While my friends and I were in Concord, Astor called but I did not answer my phone. I did not want to talk to him I was busy having fun. After he tried to call he sent me a text message that said other students had been giving him a hard time about cheating on me, and he wanted me to help him do damage control. After reading, the text message I started laughing because after all he had put me through, he had the nerve to ask me for my help. It felt good to laugh I had not felt like laughing in a long time. I decided not to respond because no matter what I said it would not matter. I also felt he was a total loser and deserved whatever he got.

After spending a little more time at the mall, we decided to head back to campus, and hang out in my room. We were watching old television reruns when my phone started ringing. I answered it without checking the caller id, which was a stupid and dumb mistake. It was Astor and he was going on and on about how he really needed my help.

He said all I had to say was I was not angry with him. I told him I was not getting involved. I felt that whatever was going on with him was his own fault and asked him not to call or text me anymore. Surprisingly Astor hung up but I was worried that that would not be the last time I heard from him. I decided that I was going to take a break from dating for a while. I focused on school and having fun with my friends. We ended up having some really amazing times together, from going skiing and snow shoeing to just taking random drives through New Hampshire and Vermont.

Seeing all the beautiful sights was amazing and I really enjoyed spending that time with my friends. One day after having a particular fun day of driving and shopping, we decided to go to the dining hall for dinner. I was starving and I hoped that the dining hall was going to be serving the garlic bread because it was one of my favorites.

When we ran intro Astor, and Sally however, I just walked right past them and find my friends. As I was looking for them, Sally decided to throw her cranberry juice at me. The juice went all over my favorite blouse. Fortunately, for me two campus safety officers saw the whole thing and took her to their office.

I went to the bathroom to see if I could get the stain out of my shirt. After dinner, I went back to my dorm and went to the laundry room to see if I could save my shirt. Fortunately, since I washed it right away the stain came right out. My friends came over to see me and see if I was okay and I told them I was just fine.

I did not want them to know that I let that skanky pathetic, rat faced bitch get to me. Unfortunately, they saw right through that and I started crying. I told them I wanted to rip her cheap and ugly hair extensions right out of her head. Michael put an arm around me and started laughing he told me that if I had done that then I would be the one in trouble.

As for Sally, she received a warning moved to another dorm, and could not have any contact with me anymore. I felt better when I realized she could not bother me anymore, but there was still the matter of the spineless jellyfish also known as my ex-boyfriend. About a week after the dining hall incident, he tried to talk to me, but I walked away from him before he could even say anything. A few went by and I decided that my friends and I needed a blowout party to let off some steam.

The party was great we were all having a blast that is until Astor decided to crash the party. I forgot to lock my door so he just walked right in and acted as if it was no big deal. He asked if he could please just talk to me but I told him I did not have anything to say. He cheated on me and because of that, we were over I could not date someone I did not trust.

After that, Michael and James grabbed him gently by his arms and escorted him to the door. I wish I could say that after that, he took a hint and left me alone but he did not. About a week after the party, I was in the library studying for a test I was going to be having in my American Lit course, the next thing I knew Astor showed up and took my American Lit book.

I grabbed it back and told him to get out of my face. He told me he was sorry but I just ignored him, grabbed my stuff and walked away. As I left the library tears were falling from my eyes, I was not paying attention to where I was going, and I tripped.

I did not want to make a scene so I quickly picked myself up and continued walking towards my dorm. Unfortunately, Astor was right behind me and saw me fall but I tried my best to ignore him. When he caught up to me, he told me his parents had paid him to go out with Sally and dump me because she was from a wealthy family and therefore was a better choice for him then I was.

When I heard that I did not even respond I just kept walking and when I got to my floor, I told him to kick rocks and suck eggs. Fortunately, after that he finally got the message that I was not interested in him anymore and left me alone. When he finally got the message, I decided to have a party with my friends. We laughed until our faces hurt. I felt grateful to have amazing friends that were always there for me through thick and thin. The rest of that semester went smoothly and I made the dean's list.

When it came time to go back home for Christmas break a part of me did not want to go. The rest of me was saying let us get out of here. When I got home, I hung out with my mom, my brother and my friends from home. When it came time to take our annual trip to Pennsylvania, I was very excited. I thought it was going to be nice to see my family again. As we drove to Allentown, I was feeling really excited and happy I could not wait to see all my relatives.

When we arrived there were hugs, a few how are you, and then we all went out to dinner. On Christmas day, my family and I opened presents, and went out to dinner. I was happy to be with my whole family again. It was also nice and special because my uncle and his fiancé were getting married that Friday.

During dinner, we pretty much talked about the wedding plans. I was going to be a bridesmaid along with her other niece Janet. The next day it was time for our bridesmaid dress fitting. When we arrived at the shop, they had our dresses ready for us. The dresses were beautiful, and I felt like a princess. I was so happy for my uncle and his amazing bride to be.

I loved her she was so nice and sweet. The day of the wedding was also beautiful. My uncle and my new aunt looked so happy. When the ceremony ended and the reception began we all danced and ate amazing food.

After the wedding, I felt like the luckiest girl in the world to be a part of this beautiful ceremony and family. As my uncle and new aunt went to leave on their honeymoon, I thought about my own wedding day and hoped it would be as beautiful and lovely as this wedding had been. When the next semester started, I made a vow that I was not going to let anyone or anything ruin the rest of my school year.

On the first night, back my friends and I were having a dance party, and everything was going great until we heard a knock on the door. It was Astor wanting to get back together. I actually laughed for a split second before I calmly told him, that I did not love him anymore. After all, I could not love someone I did not trust. He got angry but I did not care I closed my door and went back into the party. I could hear him stomping down the hall but I did not care.

He was not worth my time or energy anymore. Instead of dwelling on Astor, I decided to focus on having fun with my friends and enjoying my first night back at school. We dance and danced until we had no energy left. We were having a blast, and I felt that this semester was probably going to be the best semester ever. It felt so great to be back with my friends, I had really missed them. As the party wrapped up my friends said goodbye and I closed my door.

After everyone left, I cleaned up and went to sleep, that night I had the strangest dream. I was five years old again and I was with my imaginary friend Aries Star. Together we were traveling through a jungle and discovering the amazing plants that lived there. Suddenly a huge rainstorm hit the jungle and we had to find shelter.

We ran and ran until finally; we saw a cave and we hid there until the storm went away. I started to laugh and then

I wished that I was I was still five years old in real life. Aries laughed and told me that it was a silly wish. I started to tell her everything I had been through, and she put a cold hand on my shoulder. She told me she would always be there for me whenever I needed her. When I woke up, I felt strange; however, I had little time to dwell on it since I had to get ready for class. I quickly got dressed, brushed my hair and ate breakfast. After I had completed all of that, I grabbed my books and headed out the door, and locked the door to my dorm room behind me.

When class started, I had a hard time concentrating because I could not stop thinking about my dream. After my classes were over for the day, I went back to my room and took a nap. When I woke up, I made dinner and then watched a movie. However, sometimes I will admit that I did think about Aries but I was too old to talk to her. I had stopped believing in imaginary friends a long time ago.

I told myself get a grip you are in college now for god's sake, what kind of college student still believes in imaginary friends. I decided it was time for me to move on. To take my mind off the ridiculous dream, I decided to hang out with my friends. We watched movies and ate a lot of junk food. After a few days, I felt better and forgot all about the weird dream. When exams rolled around I did really well, I was somewhat glad the semester was over I was homesick.

When I went home, I spent time with my family and my friends. For the first time in a long time, I felt like my old self again. I was relieved that it was my summer break and for the next three months, I was home. I did not think about school or Astor at all. I just thought about going to the beach, the mall and all of my other favorite places. I kept it touched with Sarah and the crew, but I also spent some time alone, just thinking and relaxing.

By the time it was time for school to start, I was ready to go back. I spent that semester focused on school and taking every opportunity that came my way. I was in Easton dorm in a renovated single that came with a couch and I felt like I was living large. My friends were living in apartments but I loved living in my dorm and I had them over a lot. We would study and have wild and crazy parties. When it came time to celebrate my birthday, my friends and I went all out.

We had a great party complete with food, alcoholic beverages, ice cream and of course birthday cake. When my friends birthdays came around we celebrated them with style too. Every day that year felt like a party. I had the best year I had ever had since I first came to the college. For the rest of that year I stayed focus on school and made the dean's list.

The following year was probably one of the most intense years I spent at school. I had made some new friends that I would hang out with when I was not hanging out with my other group. Nick, Bertha, Martha, Louise Clark, Bradley, Beatrice, Zachary, and Casey were at the time some of my closet friends. However, Sarah Michael, James and Chester were my main crew. Nick and his crew did not like Sarah, Michael, James or Chester so since I did not want anyone to feel left out; I tried to spend time with both groups.

I would party a lot with Sarah and the gang and I guess that made the other group jealous, especially Bertha and Martha. In fact, because of my partying and having fun, they took it upon themselves to send a message to all of their friends about it. The only weird part about it was their friend's did not really know me. They also sent it to RAs who called me in for a formal sit down. They told me they were concerned about my partying and if it continued to get out of control, they were going to have to call a meeting with my counselor and get me help.

I started yelling and told them they could go fuck themselves, then my area coordinator told me to calm down. I told her to fuck off too and ran out of the room. I was so furious I could feel my face burning up. I ran all the way to my room and slammed the door. I stayed there for the rest of the day. I cried and cried until I felt that I had no tears left.

After a few minutes, I heard my phone go off. It was a text from Sarah she was coming to get me and I was to pack a suitcase and meet her outside in ten minutes. Even though I was a little confused about what was going on, I quickly packed a suitcase and went outside to wait for Sarah. When Sarah arrived, she was in the car along with the rest of the crew. They told me to put the suitcase in the trunk and get in the car, so I did.

As we were pulling away, I kept asking Sarah where we were going all she would say was we were going away for the weekend. James and Michael grabbed my hands and told me everything was going to be okay. I was unsure what was going on but I decided to go along with it because after all these people were my friends they would never do anything to hurt me.

 We drove until we arrived at a bunch of lake houses. After parking the car, Sarah went up to the biggest one, opened the door, and told the rest of us to unload the car. Sarah smiled and told us we would be staying here for the weekend. I could not believe how lucky we were; this looked like it was going to be an amazing trip.

 As we walked toward the house, Sarah told us that we could not use our cell phones while we were there, so we all called our parents and then turned them off. We quickly unpacked and then went to a nearby grocery store to buy food for the weekend. I was amazed at how much fun we were going to have and for the first time in a while, I felt safe. The lake was so serene and peaceful l I felt that I was on the vacation of a lifetime. That afternoon we spent the day laying out in the sun getting a tan and just relaxing and enjoying each other's company.

 After we laid out in the sun for a while, we played volleyball and had a picnic lunch. At dinner that night, we had a real feast, hotdogs corn on the cob and potato salad. We ate like kings and queens. After dinner, we played truth or dare, watched a few movies, had a bonfire and then went to bed. When everyone went to sleep, I caved and turned on my cell phone. I could not help myself. However, once I had turned it on I wish I had not. There were at least a hundred and fifty texts, a hundred missed calls, and fifty voicemails.

 I did not answer any of them; I just turned it back off

and went back to bed. I told myself I would deal with that mess when I got back to school for the moment; I was going to enjoy this mini vacation with my friends. I closed my eyes and then the next thing I knew Sarah was waking me up for breakfast. The next day we all just hung out and laughed and hung out around the lake. I had not felt like laughing in a long time so it felt good to laugh. I felt like finally it was okay to be myself and not worry about what others thought of me.

We were having so much fun; I did not even think about school. We were having a great time together away from school just letting our hair down and relaxing. That night was much like the first except we made brownies and ate too much candy. As the sun set in the sky and I closed my eyes for the first time in a long time I felt safe and happy. Being at the lake house was just what we all needed. It gave us a chance to relax and recharge. The lake house was a great vacation but we had to go back so we did.

When we got back to school, I went to my room and unpacked. After I was all unpacked and put my dirty clothes in my hamper, I decided to turn my phone on. I called my mother and let her know we got back to school safely.

After talking to my mom, I read all the texts, and listened to the voicemails. Some of the voicemails were a little scary. The texts were even stranger, most of them were from my ex friends, the busybody resident assistants and campus security staff.

There were also some from my brother and my friends from home. I answered them and then I decided to take a nap, which turned into a deep sleep. I slept until my phone alarm went off telling me it was time to go to class the next morning. I quickly changed into jeans and a sweater, brushed my hair and teeth and headed out the door so I would not be late.

After my classes were over, I went and found my friends. They told me that people have been asking them where we went all day. I started to panic until Sarah came up with a cover story. We all agreed that the cover story was we just needed to get away for a while, so we went on a three-day road trip and did not have service so we could not use our phones.

After hanging out for a while we went to dinner and while we were at dinner, I felt like everyone there was staring at us. People would look at us and then look away, but it was strange. I felt like a freak in a circus or something. Despite feeling like a freak, I was glad to be back on campus, I felt refreshed and ready to face anything. The trip to the lake had been just what the doctor ordered. It is funny how a trip with people you care about can make all the difference when you need to clear your head.

As people were looking at me, I was wondering what the fuss was about. People left campus all the time and no one made a fuss. However after I thought about that it made sense. People on this campus were always concerned about us. I felt bad for causing so much worry but at the same time, I felt a little outraged at the fuss. Eventually Minnie the area coordinator came up to us and asked us where we had been and what we had been up to while we were gone.

We told her the cover story and then after we finished eating we got up and left. Minnie called after us but we did not stop. We kept walking until we reached my room. No one felt we owed anyone an explanation. When we arrived, we locked the door and decided to stay there the rest of the night. People kept knocking on the door but we did not answer we just wanted a chance to get some rest after driving all day. After we were all settled we decided to watch some movies and then go to sleep. After the last movie we all fell asleep, two of us were on the beds and the rest took the floor. As we were sleeping, the resident assistants keyed into the room.

They tried to wake us up but since none of us would wake up they just left and closed the door behind them. The next morning, we all woke up and found that classes were canceled because it was a community building day. Instead of taking part in the community-building day, my friends went back to their rooms to do homework. I decided I had better do the same since I had some papers I needed to finish.

As I was working on my papers, my phone started to ring, it was Minnie and she wanted me to come to the duty office right away. I told her I was busy and could not come and then hung up. I felt a little guilty but then I realized I was an adult and I did not owe her an explanation about where I was.

After I finished my homework my friends stopped by for a visit. We were talking and laughing, when there was a knock on my door. Michael opened the door and to my dismay, it was Minnie. I walked to the door, told her there was nothing to talk about, and asked her to leave us alone. We had told her the story, but Minnie said she did not buy the story she suspected there was more to the story then we wanted to admit. After five minutes of back and forth we just decided to talk to her. We told her we just needed to get away and be by ourselves for a few days. We apologized for making people worry but we really needed time to ourselves.

Minnie asked us to come to the duty office because she had more questions and was not buying our story. We decided to go because we realized she was like a dog with a bone and was not going to leave this situation alone until she got the answers she wanted. We told her everything from start to finish and then we left.

After talking to Minnie, I felt a little better but I doubted she was going to do anything. However, I chose not to dwell on it and focus on school and my studies. For the rest of the day I hung out with my friends and tried to relax and forget about the whole thing because it really was not worth thinking about. Eventually it was time for dinner and my friends and I went to the dining hall. I was not very hungry but I decided to go anyway to keep my friends company.

We picked out our food, sat at our usual table and began to eat. Some of my ex friends asked to sit with us, but Sarah told them to get lost. They looked at me, with pleading eyes but I refused to look at them. Eventually after a few minutes, they got the message and joined the rest of their friends at their table.

For a split second, I felt like going over and apologizing but I did not instead, I reminded myself that they are the ones who spread my personal business all over social media and campus. For the rest of the time at dinner none of us really said anything. Eventually I told my friends I was not feeling well and decided to go back to my room to lay down. I did homework and then I went to bed. I felt just as bad the next morning but I still went to classes and my counseling session but skipped dinner. By the time the weekend came around again, I was even worse. I was throwing up but I did not have a fever.

I had this before and knew it would last for a few days so I decided to take it easy. I went to classes and did my homework but did not go to counseling or dinner. Eventually I got better and resumed my usual routine. After I got over being sick, I thought things were going to work out and my ex friends would find someone else to pick on but sadly, that did not happen. My ex friends wanted to be my friends again which shocked me because I thought they hated me.

On that day, I was in my room working on some homework when I heard a knock on my door. When I opened the door my heart sank inside my chest, because it was Bertha and Martha.

"Um hi Bertha and Martha look whatever you want to talk about I don't have time, I'm really busy right now working on homework."

"Look Gracie we realize that we went about this situation with your drinking all wrong."

"We never should have spread your personal business on social media."

"I appreciate the apology but why are you here?"

"We are here because we want you to forgive us and be friends with us and the rest of the group again."

"Wow okay well I am sorry but I can't be friends with people I don't trust."

"You guys really hurt me and you don't really seem to understand that."

"When I found out about what you said about me on social media, and it also caused a lot of problems."

After saying what I had to say, I closed my door and tried not to cry. I hoped that would be the last I would hear from those meddlesome troublemakers but it was not. Things got really awful and rumors about my friends and I began to spread like wildfire. If that was not bad enough I started getting several email messages telling me to kill myself. It got so bad that I could not take it anymore and made a terrible mistake that almost cost me my life.

It was an abnormally chilly spring day, and I had just gotten out of my classes for the day. I went to the river, took my socks and shoes off, and stepped into the icy cold water and stayed there until I heard Sarah scream. They pulled me out of the water and I was as cold as an ice cube. Once I was out of the water, I could feel my heart pounding my chest and my arms and legs felt numb. In fact, I could not feel anything from my waist all the way down to my feet.

My friends were concerned about me so they called 911 and I went to the hospital. At first, I did not want to but since my friends were willing to go with me, I felt a little better. A few minutes go by and the ambulance arrives. After a few minutes, I spoke to the EMTs and then they spoke to my friends. After speaking to us, we all climbed into the ambulance. Before we left, we realized that someone was going to have to stay behind due to there not being enough seatbelts. Michael decided he would stay behind so Sarah, James and Chester could go with me.

 During the ambulance ride, I laid down on the stretcher and Sarah and Chester sat with me while James sat next to the driver. As we were riding along Sarah and Chester held my hands and tried to keep me awake. I tried to stay awake but I felt like I was a million miles away. One of the EMTs asked me basic health questions and I answered them to the best of my ability.

 When we arrived at the hospital, my friends were right by my side. After we arrived at the hospital emergency room, I was lying flat on the stretcher; and the EMTs pushed me into a small room until the doctor could see me. After a few minutes, I rolled off the stretcher and landed on the bed.

 After the EMTs left, a nurse came in the room, and asked my friends to leave the room so I could change into a gown since my clothes were soaking wet. Once my friends had left and I was in a gown I got back into bed and the nurse placed some warm blankets on top of me and told us a doctor would see me soon. Once she left, my friends came back in the room and each sat on a side of the bed and grabbed my hands. I felt better already just knowing that my friends were with me and I was going to be able to get some help. I felt so stupid and knew there was probably going to be hell to pay when we got back, but I decided that I was going to have to deal with that later.

When the doctor finally arrived, he was nice and kept asking me how I was feeling. After he ran some tests, he told me if my friends had not gotten to me when they did, I would have gone into hypothermic shock and died. I was grateful to my friends for saving my life but I knew I was going to be facing a tough road ahead.

When we got back to campus, we went to bed and tried not to think about what we had just gone through. While I was sleeping, I thought about how lucky I was to be alive and how I was never going to do anything that stupid or reckless ever again. The next day everyone was talking about what happened and at times it was hard for me to deal with all the stares and whispers but I did my best.

What really helped was through it all my friends stayed right by my side and gave me all the support I needed to get through this rough patch. Unfortunately, even the support of my friends would not help me get through the meeting I had to sit through, with the associate dean of students. I hated the associate dean of students Jack Dickerson from the moment I met him, because he was an egotistical jackass and that was the nice way of putting it. He had gray curly hair and these creepy big eyes and a weird shaped nose. When I went into the meeting he told me, I was a selfish drama queen and I needed to learn to deal with my problems in a healthier less attention seeking way.

After hearing that I lost, it and I let him have it by the

end of the meeting he apologized to me but I was still angry. I told him directly that I was going to do my best to graduate and get as far away from the school as humanly possible. He told me not to be so dramatic and then said I could go so I did. After the meeting, I decided it was time to try to take a deep breath and do my best to do whatever it took to get through senior year without any more issues or drama.

I knew that was going to be tricky but I also knew I did not have a choice, unless I wanted to have to pay another visit to the hospital. Nothing was going to force me to deviate from my path, I was going to graduate and then I was going to go back home and figure out what my next step should be. I focused on my classes and kept my eye on the shiny graduation prize.

Throughout the next few weeks, my friends kept a very close eye on me because they did not want to lose me. I felt grateful to have them by my side but at times, I felt slightly embarrassed by all the attention. I knew that I was lucky to be alive but I also wished that the rest of the year would go by quickly and without any more incidents. I hoped that people would realize that I was trying my best to stay strong and just let me deal with things in my own way and for the most part, they did.

As for Bertha and her cronies, they continued to bully me but I did not let them get to me. When the school found out about the harassment, they moved Bertha and her pathetic followers away from my dorm. I thought my troubles were behind me and I was not going to have to talk about this issue anymore, but I was wrong. Minnie kept on asking me to talk and I told her I was not ready; I was not sure if I would ever be ready to talk about this. I was grateful to my friends for saving me but I still felt depressed. My friends and I decided stick together and have fun. We continued to party but we did it responsibly and made sure things remained calm and quiet.

Things were going really well until my birthday. Since my birthday fell on a weekend, we decided to go to the lake house and have a three-day sleepover-birthday extravaganza. While I was packing my ex, friends decided to come to my room and start pounding on my door, I ignored them and continued to pack everything I was going to need on the trip.

When they decided to start trying to pry my door open, I finally lost my temper. I opened the door, told them to leave me alone and if they continued to harass me, I was going to call campus security. After that, they finally left me alone and I left. Eventually my friends arrived and I got in the car and we were on our way to the lake house. I was excited because I was going to be celebrating my special day with my amazing friends. The party was amazing and the three-day celebration was amazing. To be honest I do not remember most of it not that I am proud of it. This birthday was special and when we drove back to campus, I felt the best I had felt in a long time.

When I went back to my room there were some notes taped to the door. When I grabbed them and I read them, my heart grew three sizes. The notes were sweet birthday messages from people in my dorm. As I read them, I felt like the luckiest girl in the world, I had no idea I had so many people who were willing to make me feel special on my special day. I decided that for the rest of my time at school I was going to have fun and stay positive and strong. I tried to enjoy my time at school as much as I possibly could because I knew that my time at Water Crest College was ending.

I was not sure how I felt about it, but I knew it was time and I was ready to face the world with all the strength and courage I would need to get through it. When the last few days before the ceremony finally arrived, I cleaned out my room, said my goodbyes and prepared for the next phase of my life. When the day of the ceremony arrived, I put my graduation dress on, fixed my hair and put on my cap, gown and shoes.

When I was ready, I took a final look in the mirror to make sure I looked perfect for the ceremony. After I made sure I was ready to go, I walked outside to wait for my ride to the bridge. After a few minutes, my Uncle Marcus and Aunt Wilma pulled up in their pickup truck and drove me to the bridge. When I got out of the car, I found my friends; we lined up and waited for the ceremony to begin. Finally, after what seemed like forever the ceremony was starting. When we arrived inside the ice arena, I looked up and saw my family waving at me so I waved back.

After the two-hour ceremony, it was finally time to say final goodbyes and check out of my dorm room. As I walked out of the arena, I stopped and took pictures with my friends. I checked out of my room said my goodbyes and then jumped into the car. As we pulled away, I blew a kiss to the dorm and said goodbye to Water Crest College. As we drove away from my dorm, I could not help but feel a little melancholic. I was glad to be going home but I was going to miss my friends.

The drive back home was eventful to say the least. As we were driving, we stopped to get gas and a man cut my mom off when she tried to pull up to the first available pump. She honked at the driver, pulled into the next available spot pumped the gas, and gave the driver the middle finger. The driver gave her the middle finger too and then my mom yelled at him and got back in the car.

When we arrived back home, my family decided to hang out for a while and give me some of my graduation presents. My mother and brother's gift was the biggest gift of all a redone bedroom complete with a new bed set and color of paint on the walls. I was stunned when I first saw it because it did not look like the same room. However, I was also thrilled because it looked like an adult's room and not a little kid's room.

My aunt and uncle gave me a star statue with reach for the stars engraved on it; a star a necklace with my name and the year I graduated. They also gave me money that I promised to spend wisely. After a few hours, it was time to get ready to go to my party. Before we could leave, my mom went to get the cake out of the fridge and she accidently hit a beer bottle, causing it to smash into pieces onto the floor. Sensing that my mother wanted to be alone to clean up the mess, my aunt grabbed the cake from my mom and we all left for the restaurant.

My friends Ann, Marsha and Leslie were already there waiting for us. We got a table and my mom showed up a few minutes later. We ordered nachos and our meals and then it was time to sit, relax, and catch up with everyone. I was so joyful to be home with my friends and my family. I had missed everyone a lot while I had been gone. When the food arrived it was a real feast, and I felt like the most important college graduate in the world. After the party, we all said our goodbyes and my family went back to my mom's house.

As I got ready for bed, I thought about how relived and happy I was to be home with my family and friends. I could not wait to see what the summer had in store. I was missing school a little bit, but I hoped with time that feeling would go away, and it did eventually.

Graduate School and A New Relationship

Dear Diary,

    A few months of summer went by and then it was time for me to start graduate school. By this point, I was still keeping in touch with my college friends but it was harder. We were not seeing each other every day so the emails became less and less frequent until the just stopped all together. I was going to attend the prestigious business program at Masonville University. I enjoyed graduate school and for my first few courses, I received straight A's, which shocked me because the work was much harder than it was during undergrad but it was worth it. I was proud of my accomplishment and looked forward to what lay ahead.

    A few months later, I found out my brother who had recently moved out, decided to purpose to his girlfriend Martha. I was so happy and excited I could barely speak. The day that

    Jason purposed, she said yes and they began planning their wedding right away. Martha asked me to be a bridesmaid so I gratefully accepted, that is until I saw the hideous puffy pink dress I had to wear.

    However, I was still in the wedding because I thought it would be rude of me to bail on them at the last minute. The wedding was something out of a fairy tale it was beautiful and classy. The decided to have the wedding, at a local country club. The day of the wedding was crazy and hectic, everyone was trying to finalize details and make sure that Jason and Martha had the perfect wedding. Personally I didn't get what all the fuss was about but I decided to just go along with it and help when I was needed, and when I wasn't needed I stayed out of the way.

    When it came time to walk down the aisle I walked slowly with my brother's friend Jack holding my arm. As we reached the end of the aisle and I saw the dopey look on my brother's face, I knew he had found his soul mate. After the ceremony, we went to Starflakes, which was a new fancy restaurant near the venue. When we all walked into the ballroom it was decorated with beautiful orange and pink orchids and blue and gold ribbons. A part of me felt overwhelmed but also excited for my brother and new sister in law.

    Martha was really sweet and thoughtful and I liked having her in the family even if it meant having to share my brother with her. I knew that even though Jason was married he would always have time for his adorable sister. As the evening went on my brother asked me to dance and I said yes.

"Well I guess I'm a married man now."

"I guess so but I'm still your number one sister right?"

"Yes and I still love you the same amount as I always have, and I will always be there for you."

"I love you the same amount too and I will always be there for you too."

I loved dancing with my brother and when it was over, I smiled and walked over towards the bar, and ordered a cocktail. As the evening winded down and the guests started leaving, I started to picture what my own wedding was going to be like. I had not really thought about dating since I broke up with Astor but I thought not every man is like Astor. There were decent men out there that are really sweet and thoughtful. As the wedding ended, I thought about finding my own perfect man. I was about to find him and when I did nothing was going to be the same.

A few months went by and I had new friends named Wanda Jerkinson and Darla Quirkerson. We did everything together, shopping, going out for dinner, and even went clubbing a few times. I also had a new boyfriend his name was Blaze Amethyst he was a photographer and had his own photography business. I fell in love with him because he showed me a side of the world that was flawless and beautiful. I loved him and he was always doing goofy things to make me smile and laugh.

When I introduced him to my family, they loved him, except for Jason. Jason gave him the third degree, which was somewhat embarrassing but I knew it was because my brother was only trying to protect me. However, after a few weeks of getting to know him better, Jason decided, Blaze was good enough to date me. When he told me he approved me laughed and told him while I appreciated, his approval I would have kept seeing Blaze whether he approved or not. He laughed and gave me a hug.

A few months later Martha was pregnant and had a

beautiful little girl Ella Rose Paris. I was excited to be an aunt but I could not help but feel a little jealous of her too. Ella Rose was beautiful, and every time I babysat her, I did not want to give her back. To make it easier to give her back I kept telling myself that someday I would have kids of my own with Blaze and we would be an amazing and perfect family.

As the weeks went by Blaze and I got closer and closer, and I knew that, my vision of having kids with this man was going to come true. I loved him and his spontaneity; he was always surprising me with special trips to London and Paris and other various places. I loved traveling with him and seeing the world with a whole new prospective.

Everything was perfect with Blaze and he made me happy. He was a great person and extremely kind and considerate of others. He was the kind of man that went out of his way to help people, even if he did not know them he would try to help. I could not believe how lucky I was to have found such an amazing person to spend time with that loved me for me.

Blaze never tried to change me or belittle me and when I told him, I had Asperger's Syndrome he told me he did not care. He was the type of man I had always dreamed of; we had a strong connection that I had not had with any other man I dated. We trusted each other and I could always be honest with him, even if what I said was not what he wanted to hear. Wanda and Darla liked him too, but they also thought that we were getting too serious too fast. One day we had a huge fight about Blaze and I thought it was going to be the end of our friendship. It started like any other night with my friends, but it gradually took a turn for the worst.

"Look Gracie it's not that we hate Blaze it's just that we think you guys are way too young to be thinking about marriage and having babies."

"I never said we were thinking about marriage and having babies."

"Well not in so many words but it is kind of obvious you want to have those things with him."

"What is so wrong about wanting to plan for a future?

"Blaze and I are just two people who love each other and want to be together, what's so horrible about that?"

"Nothing it's just he takes up quite a bit of your time."

"What's that supposed to mean, you think I am spending too much time with Blaze?"

"What we mean is you hardly ever go out with us and when you do, Blaze almost always tags along."

"He's my boyfriend and he likes hanging out with you guys.

At this point, I was getting wrathful and defensive these two were supposed to be my friends, and they were acting like jealous teenagers.

"That's great it's just that it would be nice if we could go out without him once and a while just the three of us, like we used to before he came into the picture."

At this point, I was done, and I said something I did not mean but they pushed me too far. I was wrathful, and I was tired of these too criticizing my relationship with Blaze.

"Whoa it sounds to me like you two are jealous because I have a boyfriend and you two don't."

"Well if that's how you feel then maybe we should take a break from each other for a while."

"Maybe we should, call me when you two get over yourselves."

After that, I did not speak to them for a month, and then I called them and apologized. After talking for a few minutes, we were all laughing and it felt like things were going to be okay. Later on that night, we went out to dinner just the three of us. They agreed to stop being so critical of my relationship with Blaze and I agreed to tell Blaze that we needed girl time sometimes.

Fortunately, when I talked to Blaze about this he was fine with it and agreed to give my friends and me some space. He actually came up with the idea that while I was having my girls' night with my friends he could have a night with his male friends. Everything was falling into place and I was relieved to have my friends back. I felt so lucky to have a boyfriend that respected my space, we did not always have to be together but it was always special when we were.

A few years later, I was running my own design store called Finnersons and Blaze was still taking pictures but kept dreaming of expanding his business. I loved having my own store and being my own boss. Fortunately, Blaze was supportive of me and together Blaze and I made an interesting couple. We loved each other and traveled the world together, when I was with him nothing seemed impossible.

Everything was always wild and exciting with Blaze. It did not matter to me what we did as long as we were doing it together. I thought I had it all, a great man, an awesome career, and a wonderful family and group of friends. I did not think I could ever be more content then I was that day. However I could not have been more wrong, I was about to get a whole lot happier than I ever thought was possible Blaze and I had been dating for a while, and everything was going perfectly. However right before our trip to Europe, I noticed a change in Blaze he was becoming secretive and evasive.

He was always sneaking off to places and a part of me wondered what was going on. The night before we left for Europe I asked him what was going on, and he smiled at me with that cute cheeky grin of his and told me I would see soon enough. One night while we were in

London he asked me to marry him. I was so stunned I kissed him and said yes. I was so excited I could not wait to tell my friends and family I was engaged to a kind, honest and handsome man who loved me. When I told my friends they were happy for me, however when I told my family they were a little worried and told me I was too young to get married.

I told them I was getting married and I expected them to there to support me. I also told them if they did not want to go to my wedding I would understand. My family laughed and told me of course they were coming to my wedding. Even if they thought, I was too young they still wanted to be there for me. I reached out to Sarah, Alexander, James Michael and Chester and even though we hadn't spoken in a while they decided to come to the wedding too.

When the big day finally arrived, I was so excited I could barely speak. My friends who were in my wedding party helped me put on my dress, shoes, and makeup. Finally, it was time to walk down the aisle. My brother grabbed me by the arm and together we walked down the aisle.

When we reached the end, he told Blaze, take care of her and then he kissed me on the check and walked back to his seat. When we exchanged our vows, I felt like the luckiest girl in the world. After the wedding was over, everyone headed to my father in law's restaurant for the reception.

As everyone was eating, I realized just how lucky I was to have found the man of my dreams, and I could not wait to begin the next phase of my life as Blaze's wife. Life was going to be amazing and I could not wait to go on more adventures together.

New Life in Binkabongana Island

Dear Diary,

    After the ceremony and honeymoon in Paris, Blaze and I moved to Binkabongana Island, a small island located on the western coast of Australia. At first, I did not really want to move but Blaze had received an incredible job opportunity to expand his photography business at a large photographer's studio. This was a great opportunity for Blaze but I did not want to leave America or our families and friends.

    After giving it some serious thought and consideration, I knew that if I really loved Blaze I should support him so I did. We told our families what was going on and then we told our friends. A few weeks later, we got passports and all the other documents we were going to need so we would be ready for our new life. We told my customers that we would be selling my shop and told our property owner we would be moving.

    After we got our passports and got all the other documents and necessary paperwork taken care of, we were ready for our new life to start. However, it was still hard for me to think about leaving my family and friends behind me and start over in a strange new place. I had never been to this island before, but even though it was hard I was really excited. While I was packing up our stuff in preparation for the move, I realize this was the right thing to do. It was a chance to try something new and I would not be alone I had my amazing and gorgeous stud muffin husband with me.

Moving to this new place was not going to be easy but it would be worth it. It was going to be a chance to start over and have a chance to have a new life. A few weeks later, we flew to the island, bought a house and then came back to America to move out of our apartment and say goodbye to everyone. During the last week before our big move, our family and friends decided to throw us a goodbye party. I cried threw most of the party but I still managed to have fun. After the party was over, we went back to our apartment to take care off the rest of our affairs.

The rest of that week, we had a lot to do we sold our cars, packed everything up and shipped all our gifts and belongings. Our last day and night were the hardest of all. Blaze and I decided that the party did not give us the closure we were hoping for so we had our friends and family over to say goodbye one last time.

Saying goodbye to everyone one last time was hard but it was not just saying goodbye to our friends and family that made me feel anxious and depressed I was also sad to be saying goodbye to America. Later on that night as I was sleeping, I could not help but feel a little sad about leaving and moving to a completely new country. I knew everything was going to be different but then I thought that might be a good thing.

The next day a car came to take us to the airport, when I saw the car I was shocked, Blaze laughed and told me that his boss arranged it. As we drove away, I took one last look at our apartment and then I fell asleep. Blaze woke me up when we arrived at the airport, for our fifteen-hour flight. Once we were on the plane, I started wondering what our new life on Binkabongana Island was going to be like.

    Once we got off the plane, we grabbed our luggage, got into a car and arrived at our new home. When I got out of the car Blaze told me to close my eyes, so I did he grabbed my arm and led me towards our new house. When I opened them, I saw our house had the most beautiful and luxurious furniture I had ever seen. We had new black leather couches, chairs, and a new oak stained kitchen table with matching stools.

    When I asked Blaze about it, he laughed and told me he had ordered the furniture online as a surprise for me. I was so shocked and touched I could barely speak. As I walked around and explored my new large and luxurious house, I could not help but feel a little sad and homesick for our apartment and everyone we left behind. I felt a little torn I loved our new home but I missed the apartment and our friends and family. Blaze put an arm around me and asked me if I was missing home and I told him I was a little but I was determined to make this new house and life work.

    After we unpacked all of our belongings, we went to the local grocery store to buy food for the week. The store was nice but a little overwhelming. They had every type of fruit, vegetable, and other types of food in the world there. I could not decide what I wanted so Blaze and I bought some of everything. When we got home, we had a feast to celebrate our new home and life. As we went to bed I made a vow that I would be able to get through this and be able to have a great life here with my husband.

The next day Blaze went to work and I went to look for a job. As I was walking, I came across a charming little shop that was for sale. I went inside met with the agent that was selling the property, and then I called my husband. He came over after work and after seeing how much I loved the place and its potential; he made an offer.

I was shocked I told him he had already done so much for me, but he told me he insisted. He told me that since I moved out here so he could fulfil his dream of expanding his photography business, the least he could do was buy me a building so I could have my own store.

After all the formality paperwork was finished, I decided the shop was going to be a design studio. After a few months of construction, the studio was finally ready and I had my grand opening. The whole family came and even some of our friends. A few weeks went by, and then the most amazing thing happened I made a new friend. Her name was Jessie and she had come into the store because like me, she and her husband had just moved to the island and were looking for a designer to design their house.

After I designed the house, she and I became friends and I met all her kids. After I met the kids, I could help but feel a little envious of her family. I could not wait until I had a child of my own to take care of and love. When I spoke to Blaze about this, he would just smile and tell me to be patient. He also said one day when I least expected it,

I would be pregnant with our first child.

After a week, my brother called me and told me Martha was pregnant again and he asked if I would come to Massachusetts for the birth and I said yes. I was so happy about the news I could not wait to meet my new niece or nephew. A few months went by and my brother called me and told me that Martha was going to go into labor soon. Blaze and I flew to Massachusetts and made it to the hospital just in time for the birth. Martha had a beautiful baby girl named Amanda Louise Paris.

When I held her, I felt like the luckiest woman in the world. However, I could not help but feel sad that I was not pregnant. I tried my best to be patient and kept myself busy with the shop and taking vacations to visit our family in America but I still really wanted a baby.

Becoming A Mother and Raising Children

Dear Diary,

    A few years later, I found out I was pregnant and I was so happy I could barely speak. When I told Blaze the exciting news, he passed out but I think it was just form shock. When he woke up he hugged and kissed me, and we both cried tears of joy. When we told our families, they were shocked but were overjoyed with the news. A few weeks later, I had a baby shower. I got many wonderful and useful gifts including a surprise visit from family and friends from America. A few months went by and I gave birth to a healthy son, named David Roland Amethyst named after my father and my mother's father. David was the perfect baby, and he stole my heart.

    When I held my son for the first time, all I could do was look at him and smile. He had dark brown eyes and dark brown hair. When Blaze saw him, he kept saying that he was going to be a scientist. I laughed and told him as long as he was healthy and happy that was what mattered. When our families arrived, they kept fighting over who was going to hold him first. After everyone had a chance to hold him and fuss over him, I told everyone his name was David Roland Amethyst, my brother thought it was a little long but everyone else seemed to like it.

I loved my son and I could not keep my eyes off him. He was so perfect and I could not believe how lucky I was. The family took many pictures and then a nurse came in and told everyone that my son and I needed our rest so they were going to have to leave. As I closed my eyes, I thought about the new chapter of my life and then I closed my eyes and went to sleep.

I wish I could tell you that adjusting to life with a baby was a piece of cake but it was not, being a new mother was tough. David was a very needy baby, and he did not sleep well. Every few hours one of us had to get up and take care of him. One night he would not stop crying so I got in my car and drove him around for a while, until he fell asleep. As I drove us back home, I could not help but feel shocked at how quickly my life had changed. I loved my son but I wished he would not cry so much.

A few years later shortly after David's 4th birthday, my daughter Riley Iris Amethyst came into the world. I was so happy and felt like the luckiest woman in the world because I had one of each just like I always wanted. Blaze and I were so happy and felt like nothing was going to bring us more joy then when our son and daughter were born. After the grandparents saw them they could not stop hugging them and kissing them. I felt so blessed; I finally had the little family I had always dreamed of; I could not wait to watch my kids grow up. Every day with Riley and David was special and I could not believe how lucky I was.

Jessie had been traveling when my kids were born and I could not wait for her to meet them. When I introduced

Jessie to my kids she immediately started fussing over them, and her kids kept fighting over who was going to babysit. A few weeks went by my husband and I decided we needed a night out, so we called Jessie and her husband and invited them to join us.

Their daughter Kelley babysat her siblings Anna and Callie and my two little ones. I was nervous about leaving them but everyone kept telling me to stop fussing. When we came home, the house was perfect. Kylie told me my kids were in bed asleep and her sisters were asleep on the couch. I was amazed and a little shocked at how well things had gone. I paid and thanked Kylie, and her parents for an amazing evening, said goodnight to them and they picked up their two sleeping daughters and left. After they left my husband and I went to check on our kids and found them both sound asleep.

When it came time for my kids to start school I cried because I did not want my babies to grow up. However, I was also happy because it meant that my babies were ready to face new challenges and learn new things. David loved school and thrived but Riley struggled. The school asked us to have her tested so we did and found out she had Asperger's Syndrome. When we sat her down to tell her we decided we should practice what we were going to say so she would understand. After we told her I promised her that I would do whatever it took to help her, just like my mom and dad had done for me.

After Blaze and I explained everything, she looked up at me and gave me a big hug. As the years went by our family changed a bit, I got pregnant again and this time I had another girl so I named her Elizabeth Martha Amethyst. She was so beautiful; when I saw her, I stopped breathing for a second because she astounded me. I could not believe just how blessed I was to have another little baby to love and take care of.

When Riley and David saw her, they were so excited and content to have another sibling to hang out with and they kept fighting over who was going to hold her first. After a few minutes they decided that since David was the oldest he would hold her first and then Riley would get to hold her. Seeing my kids with their baby sister made me feel proud because they were very gentle and loving towards her.

When my family saw her they all fussed over her and fought over who was going to get to hold her first. I loved being a wife and mother with all my heart, I loved watching my little angels grow and learn. Every day was a blessing and I was truly amazed at the amazing family I had. It was not always perfect and there were times where I had to discipline my children but we always forgave each other afterwards.

As time went by my kids grew up and started becoming more and more independent. After a while, David went off to college, graduated moved out and got a job working as a manager of the local pharmacy. I was so proud of him and so was the rest of the family. He was becoming a responsible adult and I was proud of how well he turned out. Even though I was proud of my son a part of me wished he had stayed my little baby boy, but I knew that was impossible I knew that all parents probably wish that their adult children were still their little babies, because it is hard to let go. However, we all realize that all children have to grow up someday.

As the weeks after David moved out went by, there was a bit of trouble ahead. About a month after David moved out, I went to the doctor and found out I had breast cancer. At first, I did not want to tell my kids or my husband but the doctor told me I could not keep it from them forever. Later on that night, I called a family meeting and told everyone what was going on. My kids cried my husband just sat on the couch next to me and gave me a hug.

Elizabeth then asked me if she and I could talk in private, I still remember what she said.

She asked me if I was going to die. I told her I was going to fight to the best of my ability, and then she asked me if she could go to her best friend Ann's house. I told her of course she could as long as it was okay with Ann's parents. She called Ann and her parents said it was okay for Elizabeth to come over. Blaze offered to drive her while I talked to Riley. Riley did not really have much to say she just looked at me and cried. I just held her and told her everything was going to be okay.

Over the next few months, I had my assistant manager Becky run the store while I received radiation and chemotherapy. While I was recovering from chemotherapy my mother came to stay with us, to help Blaze and I take care of Riley and Elizabeth. David helped when he could but his job kept him busy so I was grateful when my mom was with us. Fortunately, I went into remission and was able to salvage the store. Becky had done a wonderful job running it, and I was so grateful for her help. She was the best manager I could have asked for.

I was so happy that my store was doing well. The next few months I made sure the store kept running in fine working order and kept everything running like clockwork. My husband and kids all teased me and told me that if I did not stop to smell a rose occasionally I was going to miss life. Before I knew, it was time for Riley to go off to college. She decided she wanted to go to Water Crest and I was supportive of that. I just hoped that the people who gave me a hard time did not work there anymore.

Riley got into Water Crest College and before I knew it, it was time to move her into her dorm. When she was all unpacked and had everything, she was going to need we said our goodbye and left. As we drove home, I worried about how people were going to treat Riley.

However, she seemed happy there and would call and tell us how excited and happy she was. I was so proud of her, but I was also sad because she was all grown up and did not need me as much anymore. When it came time for her to graduate, I was so proud of her I could barely speak. She looked so beautiful and dignified when she graduated.

She already had a job working at my studio, but she told me she was not going to work there forever. She was going to work there until she got a different job, which was fine with me. I was so proud of her and a little jealous of her because I wish I had had the confidence that she had at her age. As for Elizabeth, she was going down her own path and was figuring things out one day at a time. She did not really know if she wanted to go to college. We looked at a few schools for her and she decided to go to Water Crest but unlike her sister who studied business, she was going to study art and become a photographer like her father.

Before I knew it, David was getting married to a wonderful woman name Isabel. We called my mother to come to the wedding and invited the rest of the family too. On the day of the wedding, everyone was there and I made sure that everything was perfect. After my son and daughter in law exchanged vows, I cried because the ceremony was so beautiful and moving.

We were all so emotional that we did not notice that Riley had decided to drink too much champagne. She was so drunk she started signing random songs, under her breath. David was a little embarrassed and disappointed in his little sister's behavior because according to him she promised him she was not going to drink. Everyone else found it hilarious because she was going to wake up with a nasty hangover the next day. Since Riley was drunk, I told my husband to take care of her while I went to find Elizabeth. I found her checking out the wedding cake and talking to a bartender. Once I saw that Elizabeth was okay I went to check on Riley.

My husband tried to get her to sit down but instead she ran off to find a bathroom so she could throw up. I was furious with Riley for acting that way but I figured I could talk to her about it later once she was sober and could comprehend what I was saying. After the ceremony and reception ended, David and Isabel said there goodbye and drove off to the airport to start their honeymoon and new life as husband and wife. After my son and daughter in law left my mom and the rest of the family, left and went back to their hotel. After saying goodbye to the family, I helped Riley to the car and then Blaze and Elizabeth followed suit.

When we got home, I decided to carry Riley upstairs to her old room and bed. I did not yell at her because her father and I agreed that the hangover would be punishment enough, besides she was an adult and it did not seem like it made sense to punish her anymore. I also realized she was old enough to know better and know her limits with alcohol. I know she was not thrilled about David marrying Isabel but that did not give her the right to drink so much. After thinking about it for a while, I figured out why Riley had done what she did and why she was so upset about David getting married.

David and Riley used to be close and spent a lot of time together. However, after he moved away and met Isabel that changed a little bit. He would visit occasionally but Isabel always came with him. I guess that really bothered Riley because she wanted his undivided attention. I could relate to that because that was how I'd felt when my brother got married.

Even though I understood why Riley had done what she did, I still felt I was going to have to talk to her. The next day after the wedding, I decided I was going to have a talk with Riley about all the changes that were happing in our lives. I realized I should have done it sooner but unlike

Elizabeth, Riley did not always tell me what she was thinking or feeling.

The next morning after Riley recovered from her hangover I talked to her about her behavior at her brother's wedding.

"Riley I honestly don't know what got into you last night, you should have known better."

"What was I supposed to do mom, act like I'm content and thrilled that a whore stole my brother from me?"

"Riley Rosemarie Amethyst, that is a completely harsh and unjustified thing to say."

"Isabel didn't steal David he is still your brother, it's just that now he has a wife and you have a sister in law."

"I hate her mom she is just so perfect."

"Riley you are being childish right now."

"Even if you don't like Isabel I hope you learn to for David's sake and for your own."

"If you don't accept Isabel you will be pushing David away and I know you don't want that."

After a few minutes, I started to get through to Riley and she realized that she was wrong. It was his special day and even if she did not like his new bride, she should not have acted that way. After she gave it some thought, she told me she was going to call David when he returned and apologize for her behavior at his wedding. After a while, Riley had a new career, new apartment and a new man in her life. His name was Angelo Mario and they started dating.

I liked Angelo and I thought he was the perfect man for Riley that is until I found out that he cheated on her with a woman he met at a nightclub. When Riley told me, I was angry but not nearly as angry as her father. He wanted to go over to Angelo's house and beat the crap out of him, but I told him that was not a good idea because he would only end up in jail. Instead, I took Riley shopping for some retail therapy. As we shopped, we talked about Angelo. While we were talking for the first time in a long time, my daughter asked me for my opinion.

I told her I thought she should follow her heart and do what she thought was best. When we arrived back at her apartment, we found Angelo's car in the parking lot and an intoxicated Angelo sitting on her doorstep. I went inside so my daughter could say what she wanted to say to him in private. She then asked me if I could give Angelo a ride home because she did not want him driving. After I dropped, Angelo and his car off I went to Riley's apartment and make sure Riley was okay. I found her in her room with the blankets around her.

She then asked me to do something she had not done since she was little. She asked me to tell her the story about how her dad and I had met. After I told her the story, she fell asleep. A few weeks later she met someone else named Curtis Pear. He was good to her and we could tell he loved her.

After five months of dating, he asked my husband if he could ask Riley to marry him. He gave him his permission and he asked her. She said yes. I was so excited I could not wait to attend my daughter's wedding. Elizabeth however did not take the news so well; she actually told me she was not going to the wedding. I told her oh yes she was she was going to be there for her sister. After that, Elizabeth stomped up the stairs and slammed the door to her room. At that moment, I had a flashback of what I was like at her age and laughed.

After a few minutes, I went upstairs and knocked on Elizabeth's door and we talked. She told me she did not like Curtis because she thought he was a nerd and was not good enough for her sister. I told her it was not up to her to decide if Curtis was good, enough it was up to Riley to decide that. I told her I respected how she felt but this was a special day for Riley, and that she should support her sister. After that she became very angry me and kept asking me why I never took her side in anything.

I told her I knew change was hard but life is full of changes and sometimes we just have to suck it up and deal with it. She told me she would try but she was not going to be happy about it. I decided that I would give her some time to get used to the idea. I knew that this was going to be a big change for her and eventually she would be fine.

Eventually Elizabeth was used to the idea and eventually felt happy for her sister and Curtis. The day of the wedding was beautiful, I was so happy for Riley but also sad because it meant she was going to be moving out and moving into Curtis's house. After the wedding and reception, I thought about how much things have changed.

However, I also thought about the one thing that had not changed. I still had a loving family, and loving friends and that is all that mattered. A few weeks later, Elizabeth decided to get her own apartment. I was so sad because she was my last baby but I was also proud of her. She was going to be working for me and found an apartment near the studio. After Elizabeth moved out, things changed but I was happy. I was happy that my kids were all grown up and living healthy and productive lives.

    A few weeks after Elizabeth moved out, I hadn't been feeling well so I went to the doctor and found out that the breast cancer I had had had come back. However, unlike the last time it was more aggressive and had spread to my bones.

    When I found out, I was not sure how to react or how I was going to tell my family. This was going to be intense and scary, and a part of me wanted to run away but I knew I could not do that. I had to face this and I was going to need all the love and support I could get.
"Blaze we need to call the family and have a family meeting."
"Okay but what is this about is something wrong?"
"Honey my cancer came back and it is more aggressive and it spread to my bones."
"Wow okay well I will go make phone calls and you go sit in the living room and relax."
    When everyone arrived, I took a breath and told everyone the bad news.
"I am sorry to have to have to tell you all this but my cancer has returned and the doctors aren't sure if I am going to beat it this time."
    A few minutes went by and then I looked around at my family, I was not sure what to say next. I just hoped that they would be able to support me and help me get through this.

"I am so sorry mom is there anything that we can do to help."

"Thank you for asking Riley but all you guys can do is support me and maybe watch the store with Becky for me while I go for my treatments."

"The good news is the doctors caught it early and they are doing everything they can to keep me alive and I am fighting to the best of my ability."

"Well at least the doctor caught it early."

"I am going to run the store and if you need me to make meals for you I will we all will right everyone?"

"Right!"

After our family meeting, I felt so relieved and blessed to have an amazing and supportive family. After speaking to my family, I called my mother she cried and offered to fly out but I told her not to. I did not want her to have to fly all the way out here but she insisted and she stayed with us and helped me around the house. My brother and sister in law helped by sending me funny emails and jokes. My nieces also sent me cards and let me know they were thinking of me.

When Jessie found out, she asked what she could do. After thinking about it for a minute, I asked her if she could help at the store and she said of course. As the weeks went, by I felt sick at times but having my family and friends love and support really helped me. Having them around made going through breast cancer a whole lot easier. A few months later David told us that Isabel was pregnant with twins. I was so happy I could barely stand it. I told myself that I had to stay alive so that I could see the birth of my grandchildren.

A few weeks after we found out about the pregnancy I found out the treatments worked and I was officially cancer free. I was so happy I cried. The funny thing is when I told my whole family they cried too. A few months went by and Isabel went into labor and brought two beautiful and healthy baby girls Sarah and Iris into the world.

When I held them for the first time, I could not believe how lucky and blessed we all were to have two new beautiful girls in our lives and family. At that moment I made a vow that, I would do whatever it took to stay healthy so that I could be there for my family and for my friends. Whatever we had to go through; we were going to go through it together. I knew that nothing was going to stop us from achieving our goals and our dreams. I hoped that everything would go back to being easy but unfortunately, life threw us another curveball.

A year went by and I got some bad news. Two months after Sarah and Iris's 1st birthday my mother got sick with stage 3 breast cancer. Jason and his wife, kids and grandkids had been taking care of her, but I decided to have Becky, Elizabeth and Riley watch the store so I could help them out. When I arrived in Rhode Island, everyone was grateful I was there. I loved spending time with my family and taking care of my mom. Unfortunately, her health got worse and she had to stay at the hospital. A few months after my arrival she died. I still remember our last conversation
"Honey I'm so grateful that you came to visit but you should be at home running your store and spending time with your

kids and grandkids."

"I wanted to be here with you and our family, Blaze wanted to come too but he is busy with his latest photo shoot."

"How are the kids and your two grandchildren?"

"They are all doing well here I brought you pictures of Sarah and Iris."

"Oh my goodness Gracie they're gorgeous, I wish I could be there and watch them grow up."

"You will be here mom. You'll see you are going to beat this and when you do, if you want to you can fly out to the island and see them."

"Honey I wish that were true but you can tell them all about me, and you can spoil them rotten just like I would have."

"I am so proud of you Gracie you have grown into such a strong and independent woman."

"I love you Momma."

"I love you too Gracie."

After talking to Jason and Martha, the grandkids and great grandkids, she died. When I called my husband who was at the store taking care of inventory, he got on a plane and flew to Rhode Island. My brother had us stay at his house. When I saw him, I cried and he hugged me. After a few moments of pleasantries, my brother and I made the funeral arrangements and then it came time to decide what we were going to do about my mother's house.

Jason thought I should have it for when Blaze and I retire, but we told him we were going to stay on the island and he and his wife should take the house but he did not want it. We then decided to ask all of our kids but they did not want it either. Since none of us wanted it and it was in fantastic shape we decided, we should sell it and split the money. When we were walking through the house, each of us selected items we wanted. The items we did not want were going to a local charity that helped families in need. As we looked through the stuff, I started to feel emotional but I pushed through it.

At the funeral, we all took turns going up to say a few words about my mother and then we said our final goodbyes. After the funeral, we spent some time together and then Blaze, the kids, and our grandkids flew home to our island. When we arrived at the airport, two cars were waiting for us to take us to our homes. After saying goodbye to everyone and arriving at our house, I started crying so Blaze comforted me, held me, and made feel better.

A few minutes later, we unpacked and then Blaze looked at me and pulled me into a hug. I just stood there in my husband's arms. I did not know what to say so I did not say anything. As he held me in my arms, he started stroking my hair, and then carried me up to bed. I went to bed and tried to get some sleep. I was missing my mother like crazy but I knew she was with my father and the rest of the family that had passed on so that helped a lot. The next day I went to the store and met with clients all day.

When I got home Riley was at the house with her husband. When I asked what they were doing there, Riley looked at me and cried. I looked at my daughter and I was puzzled, and then I was concerned. I was worried that something terrible had happened, so I went over to give my daughter a hug.

"Mom I don't know how to tell you this, especially since we just lost Nana but I'm pregnant."

"Oh my goodness congratulations you two, when is the baby due?"

"April 10th."

"Oh my goodness that's wonderful. Another grandchild for your father and me to love and spoil."

Riley looked at me and continued crying she was crying so much her shirt was getting wet. I did not know what was wrong so I took a deep breath and had Riley take a few deep breaths.

"Darling why are you so upset this is happy news."

"How can I be happy when we just lost Nana?"

"Honey I know how much you miss Nana; we all do but life has to go on and your Nana would want you to be happy about this."

"You are going to be an amazing mother and I am really happy for both of you."

A little while later we called a family meeting and set up a video chat call with the rest of the family. I was so excited I was jumping up and down like a jumping bean.

"Thank you all for coming, Riley has some very big and awesome news to share with you all."

"Everyone I'm pregnant, the baby will be born on April 10th."

"Yay congratulations this is amazing news."

"Do you guys know what you are having yet?"

"Not yet but we will find out in a few months, I think it is going to be a girl."

"I think it is going to be a boy, or twins."

"There is only one baby, Elizabeth at least I think it is only one baby ha-ha."

 A few months later, we had a baby shower for Riley and found out that she was going to have a daughter. Pregnancy agreed with Riley, she loved being pregnant and kept trying to figure out what to name her little girl. They went through so many names Riley told me she was worried there were not going to be any girl names left. The day after my birthday at five am my granddaughter Linda Rose Pear was born.

 When I saw her, she looked so much like her mother I cried. When Riley asked me to hold her, all I could do was look at that sweet little face and I melted. Linda was stunning she was so perfect all I could do was stare at her. Jessie surprised us and showed up for the birth with a teddy bear. I did not think she was going to come because we had lost touch with each other but she was there and we picked up right where we left off.

 When Riley brought little Linda home she was a nervous wreck. She kept worrying that Linda was too hot and then she thought she was too cold. Finally, I sat her down and told her to relax. I told her that all new mothers worry about their children, and the first child was the hardest but eventually she would get into the right routine. Linda was a perfect child and so were the twins. Every time I visited with them, I felt so lucky to have three beautiful granddaughters. The twins loved Linda and the three of them got along really well. I could not believe how blessed I was to have such a beautiful family. I still missed my mom and wished she was with us but I did not let it interfere with my life, which is what she would have wanted.

Endings and New Beginnings

A few months went by and my brother informed me that after being on the market for a while we finally had an offer on our childhood home, but not just any offer an above asking price offer. After discussing it for a few minutes, he and I chose to accept. It felt great to sell that house but I also felt a little sad about letting it go but I knew it was time. We did not want it and this way we could move on and focus on moving forward and keeping our mom in our thoughts and in our hearts.

If that was not exciting enough a few weeks, later Elizabeth announced she was engaged to a successful art gallery owner that she had been dating for months. I was stunned because she had never introduced him to the family. When she brought him over, I was stunned he was different then all the other men Elizabeth dated. His name was Bruce Applebuzzer, he owned his own art gallery and he and Elizabeth were going to open another one together after they were married. Blaze and I were speechless Elizabeth had never mentioned opening an art gallery.
"Hello Mr. and Mrs. Amethyst it's nice to meet you I've heard a lot about you."
"It's nice to meet you too Bruce and we haven't heard a lot about you."
"Well I am an artist; I used to work for my parents at their

art gallery on the south side of this island."

"After they died I took over the art gallery and now Liz and I are going to open a second art gallery together."

"I know our news comes as a shock to you both but I love your daughter and I intend to give her the best life possible."

"I am glad you love our daughter and we're sorry you lost your parents, but where do you two plan on living after your wedding?"

"We are renovating a nice traditional colonial on Midison Street."

"Wow that sounds exciting, have you two set a date yet?"

"We were thinking about getting married next summer on June 23rd."

 After a few more minutes of awkward conversation, we realized we liked Bruce and he really loved our daughter. We also realized although Elizabeth was young, she really loved him and they seemed to be a good match for each other. Even though I knew, they loved each other I could not help but feel nervous. Elizabeth was my last child and I was not ready to let her go yet. I wanted her to stay my beautiful baby girl forever but I knew that was impossible.

 A few months went by and the day of the wedding came. I was excited but melancholic at the same time because I did not want to give my daughter up. However, I knew she was happy so that helped a little. As the girls were getting ready, all I could do was stare and make sure that everyone had what they needed, and then I went to find my seat. When everyone was ready, the bridal precession began. As I watched Elizabeth walk down the aisle with her father,

I could not help but flash back to when she was a little girl and she was just learning how to walk.

After the wedding and reception were over, I said goodbye to my daughter and my new son in law and they went on their honeymoon. After the wedding Blaze and I went home.

"Are you alright darling you were awfully quiet during the ride home?"

"I'm alright dear I'm just a little tired, maybe I will go on up to bed."

"Okay I will be up shortly I just have some things to check on first."

As I walked up to bed I could not sleep, I could not help but think about all the things that had changed. When my husband came upstairs, I was already asleep so he let me rest. The next morning Blaze and I decided to go for a drive around the island. Driving around was a lot of fun and I noticed many beautiful sights that I had not really appreciated or noticed before. The two sights that caught my attention the most were the Wallerstonea Mountains and the Pineanera Forest. It was awesome spending time with my husband but I still felt a little depressed.

"Honey can I talk to you for a minute?"

"Sure what's up, what's wrong?"

"I feel like an empty nester and I am not sure what to do about it, the drive around the island helped but I still miss the sounds of our kids."

"Honey all the kids have been gone for ages now, I know that Elizabeth getting married has been hard for you but you have to adjust."

"Maybe we should sell the house since it is just the two of us now, we don't need all of this space"

"That's a good idea and a smaller house would be easier for us to maintain as we get older."

"But what about the kids how will they feel about us selling the house?"

Blaze paused for a second and then looked at me, and said

"They will be fine once we explain why we want to move they will understand."

"Tomorrow we will call a family meeting and discuss the fact that we need a smaller house, now that you and I are getting older."

The next day Blaze called everyone and told the kids and grandkids to come over to the house so we could have a family meeting

"Okay everyone here's the scoop your mother and I are selling the house."

"WHAT WHY?"

"The house has gotten to be too big and empty and tough to manage so we are going to sell the house and move into a smaller house."

"You guys don't need a smaller house, mom is just feeling depressed because we have all moved out and she is feeling like an empty nester."

"That isn't the only reason Elizabeth your father and I just think it is time to make a change so, we need everyone to grab their stuff and decide whether to get rid of it or keep it."

"Alright guys let's get to it."

It took a few days but eventually everyone collected all of their stuff and we got the house ready to sell. It was going to be hard selling the house but both Blaze and I felt that it was the right thing to do. We found our new house, which was a charming ranch style home that was exactly three blocks away from our current house. Blaze and I could not believe our good luck and made an offer and we got the house.

After finding our dream house, it was time to sell our current house. After a few months on the market, we got an offer on the house, and we accepted, and moved into our smaller home. After we moved into our new home, Blaze and I threw a housewarming party. All of our friends, family and even some of our new neighbors came and helped us celebrate our new home. After all our guest had gone home and we had cleaned up Blaze and I went to bed. As I laid in bed with my husband, I could not help but marvel at how well my life had turned out so far.

As I closed my eyes, I felt truly blessed to have such an amazing life and amazing people to share it with, and to me that made all the difference. I wish the reader of this diary all the successful and luck in the world. I hope you have many great adventures and success; however, I also want you to make mistakes and learn from them. It is okay to make mistakes as long as you learn from them and do not repeat them.

Remember you can do anything you set your mind to.

Do not let anyone stand in the way of your dreams, and reach for the stars, if you cannot reach them do not sweat it just keep stretching and eventually you will. Nothing in life is impossible, there is always a way to do something you just have to keep working at it until you figure out the best way to do it. Be strong, be brave and always have a smile and sunshine in your heart, even if you feel like crying.

It is okay to cry; crying is not a sign of weakness it is a valid emotion and eventually you will feel better. I hope by sharing my story I have given you some faith and confidence to always push yourself and always work hard even if other ignoramuses are telling you to give up. They are just dumbasses and you are smart; you are talented and you are awesome.

I hope that you realize even though life is complicated and messy it is amazing. Take every opportunity that comes your way, except ones that you think are dangerous those you might want to think twice about. You can and should take some risks in life but remember there is a huge difference between taking a risk and being reckless. Good luck in all that you chose to do with your life, take care of yourselves, your friends, you family and your furry friends.
All my love,
Gracie Elizabeth Paris- Amethyst

About the Author

Author Rachel R. Reichl London was born in Providence Rhode Island at Woman and Infants Hospital. She was raised in Smithfield Rhode Island and still lives there with her mother, and her three loveable pets Murphy, Nellie and Whisper. As an autistic author Rachel wants others to realize that nothing is impossible. All you have to do is want something enough to make it happen and not expect others to do it for you.

Milton Keynes UK
Ingram Content Group UK Ltd.
UKHW020724161023
430691UK00005B/44